HOLDING ONTO HOPE

HOLDING ONTO HOPE

P.I.V.O.T. LAB CHRONICLES™ BOOK EIGHT

MICHAEL ANDERLE

LMBPN Publishing
PMB 196, 2540 South Maryland Pkwy
Las Vegas, NV 89109

First US Edition, January, 2021
(Previously published as a part of the Megabook, *No Time To Quit*)
eBook ISBN: 978-1-64971-443-5
Print ISBN: 978-1-64971-444-2

THE HOLDING ONTO HOPE TEAM

Thanks to the JIT Readers

Billie Leigh Kellar
Dave Hicks
Deb Mader
Diane L. Smith
Jeff Eaton
Jeff Goode
John Ashmore
Kelly O'Donnell
Kerry Mortimer

If I've missed anyone, please let me know!

Editor
The Skyhunter Editing Team

CHAPTER ONE

"Can I ask you something?" Dr. DuBois startled Nick, who hadn't heard him approach.

"Hmm?" He looked at the doctor.

"What are you nervous about?" the man asked him. He popped a piece of caramel corn in his mouth and chewed. As far as anyone on the PIVOT team could tell, he lived entirely on popcorn. If he ever ate anything else, they hadn't seen it. What was almost more impressive was how he managed to stay so thin when he never seemed to be without a bag of popcorn in his hand.

No, the young engineer decided after a moment, the *most* impressive part was that the entire lab was not coated in cheese dust and caramel stickiness. That was the most impressive and certainly most welcome part.

He returned to the matter at hand. "I started a rumor that Jacob was dating one of the Diatek lawyers to make him and Amber realize they're still into each other. They dated in college and it fell apart, but they've both grown up since then. Anyway, they discovered yesterday that I'd started the rumor and I'm still waiting to see if they'll kill me when they come in."

"Ah," DuBois said. With his usual blunt honesty, even at his own expense, he added, "I don't see how that rumor would lead to them dating."

"Amber realized she had feelings for Jacob because she didn't like the idea of him dating someone else," he explained. "So she began to up her game with how she dressed and *Jacob*—you know, you probably don't care."

"I care," the man said, offended. "However, I will probably not understand even if you explain it. I tend to not understand these things."

He didn't seem bothered by it, but Nick was worried. "Does that bother you?"

"Not really," the doctor said cheerfully. "It's an excellent thought puzzle, for one thing. If I don't have anything else to think about, I can always think about social interactions."

"Ah." He smiled in bemusement. He was debating how to ask if he had ever dated when the door swung open and his two partners entered. His body froze and he gave them a wide-eyed look, all his senses on high alert.

"Relax," Amber said. "We've decided not to kill you."

"Right now," Jacob clarified. He put a bag of donuts on the table. "The current lack of violence should not be construed as a binding legal agreement to continue in the same manner, however, and may end at any time we see fit."

"I don't think that's how the laws around assault work," Nick said.

"It's not? Damn." The other man took a sip of his coffee. "Well, at least I have coffee and donuts to get me through this trying time."

"It does blunt the pain," Amber agreed. "Would you like a donut, Captain?"

At first, DuBois had simply been "DuBois," but as the team grew to know him better, they had learned that he loved nicknames. Obligingly, they had come up with new ones at regular intervals, and this was the newest one. It played off his first name, Jean-Luc, which he shared with a certain *Star Trek* character.

He smiled happily at the nickname and waved his bag of popcorn. "None for me, thank you."

She nodded in response and chose a donut. "So. What do we have on the docket for this week?"

Nick pulled down the whiteboard from the corner that they used for the weekly schedule. At the bottom was a complex series of colored dots representing the shifts of medical staff who were always present to tend to the patients in the facility. It was one of the many things that had become exponentially more complicated when PIVOT had received the publicity and funding to expand their baseline testing a few months earlier.

Once, it had been easy to stay on top of everything. Now, they needed weekly briefs and debriefs—or, as Jacob called them, "briefs and boxers"—and the whiteboard had become their most important office purchase.

"Jamie Mattis will arrive later today to go into the game." He began to write. "Him meeting up with his sister in the game is our next step to start moving her toward consciousness. We've been in contact with her doctors, who think she's probably ready for it—they speculated that she would be when she asked to see other people. But this is all still guesswork. None of the doctors have come across any other cases of this before."

"How are Dr. P's recommendations dovetailing with theirs?" Amber asked.

This was the language they had decided to use to refer to Prima without tipping anyone in the lab off that they were discussing a sentient AI.

"Very closely," Nick told her. "Although she usually suggests things first."

"It seems like we've had good results simply blanket approving anything they all recommend," DuBois added.

"Okay. Jacob?"

Jacob nodded. The most cautious of the group in this regard, he was slowly coming around to viewing Prima as an ally.

"Okay." Nick drew a blue line to indicate Jamie's presence in the game. "The Mattises have agreed to put Jamie into the game with the expectation that it will be for an extended period, maybe up to a week, so we'll do the whole suite of medications. I have Kevin and Augie penciled in to prep him."

Everyone nodded.

"Now, as regards Ben," he said. "Every one of his doctors is on board with continued time in the game. The progress they've seen is astounding, frankly, and his muscle tone isn't going down as quickly as they would expect. We're still waiting on the recommendations of how to cycle in-game time with out-of-pod time for building strength, but until we get those, we'll simply keep him in indefinitely."

"Cool," Amber said. "It *was* nice to see him up and about, and even him getting him back into the pod was easier than the last time."

Everyone nodded.

"What's coming up for him in terms of the story?" Jacob asked. "I've been focused on Taigan's data so I haven't seen that."

"We'll give him a story choice between a couple of different ways to learn more fine motor control," Amber answered. She and DuBois had taken the lead on this project. The team agreed that the first story Ben had gone through had been more extreme than they had anticipated.

They wanted to make sure that this time, he knew he had people he could rely on—and that his choices would reverberate on a smaller scale.

"The best in-game class for this is obviously rogue," she continued. "Having to move quietly and carefully, wielding small weapons, and doing things like picking locks or pickpocketing will all create opportunities for Ben to increase his fine motor skills."

The doctor swallowed his mouthful of popcorn. "And it will give us a chance to see if he experiences the same boost to fine motor control that he did to major motor control."

Jacob nodded agreement.

"He's on a ship to Heffog right now," Amber said. "We got that zone online barely under the wire, but it's ready now. He's learning from Zaara, and he'll meet up with one of her acquaintances there, which will allow him to trust them. Meanwhile, being a rogue and picking pockets for fun should allow him to have a more light-hearted story. After all, one of the cool things about the game is that you can do stuff that wouldn't be ethical in the real world."

"Oooh, we should have him do an *Ocean's 11* heist scenario," Jacob said with a grin.

"That could be fun," she agreed. "Plus, we could watch *Ocean's 11* again. For research, of course. It's work."

The others all grinned in approval.

"Is there anything else about Ben?" Nick asked them all.

"Oh." DuBois looked up. "I meant to say I received an email the other day from an acquaintance of his, a man named Mike."

"The other one who was in the accident?" he asked.

"I think so. He simply mentioned that, as Ben is doing better than anyone expected, he would appreciate any efforts we can make to have him in good shape to attend a wedding this fall. I guess everyone had assumed he wouldn't be able to make it but since he's doing so well, they're hoping he can."

"Okay." Amber thought about it for a moment. "I agree, it wouldn't have seemed at all possible a couple of weeks ago, but it does seem like it might be now."

"He also requested we not tell Ben this," the doctor added.

"It'll make a nice surprise."

"Maybe, but his exact words were that Ben is—and again, I quote—a 'stubborn bastard' who will make himself miserable trying to exceed the training goals if he knows about them. Mike believes it will be better for his stress level if he tries to get better for his own sake, not for the wedding. He thinks Ben might injure himself by training too hard."

"That's…" Amber looked at Ben's pod. "Probably accurate, honestly. Okay, we won't tell him. It'll be a surprise. We'll want to keep that in mind when we get word from the PT about cycling him in and out."

"I'll email him with those dates," DuBois said. "He might as well know now that it's a goal and he can weigh in."

"Good call." She smiled and finished her donut. "Okay, let's get to it."

CHAPTER TWO

The *Wind Dancer* was a gorgeous vessel. In a world full of magical possibilities such as cities carved from one block of stone, it was surprisingly wonderful to have a ship made of wood. The creak of the beams and the snap of the sails paired perfectly with the slap of the waves and the sound of gulls. Every beam was lovingly smoothed and varnished, the ship clearly both old and well cared for.

Unfortunately, Ben was able to enjoy none of this, as he had spent the past two days heaving his guts out over the side. It was a surprisingly good core workout, but he was long past the point of appreciating silver linings.

After the latest bout of vomiting, he swished water around in his mouth, spat it over the side, and said to Prima, "I *still* think it's bullshit. It isn't even a real boat."

"That's debatable. Given that you perceive the boat—"

"No," he said emphatically. "No philosophy." He looked sharply at the gathering clouds. The weather had been fair when they left port but the wind had picked up overnight and there was the sense that rain could come at any time.

"So, to be clear, you would prefer that I do not refute your factual inaccuracies?"

"Yes."

"Then what is the point of conversing?"

"I don't know," he said muzzily. He tried pushing off his forearms, which turned out to be a mistake. "Oh, hell." He narrowed his eyes at the sky when he managed to drag in a breath and settle the queasiness, at least for now. "This can't be good for my health, you know."

"Ah."

"That's all you're going to say?"

"I was instructed not to refute factual inaccuracies. This impedes my ability to respond."

Ben rolled his eyes and stumbled to the pile of rope he'd spent most of the past two days seated on. He had learned the hard way that if he didn't keep the horizon in sight, the seasickness became far worse.

He was still there, his gaze fixed resolutely on the whitecaps and the horizon, when Kural and Zaara stepped onto the deck—along with a waft of food-scented air that made his stomach heave.

Everyone else had been having a nice lunch. He wasn't sure those existed in his world anymore.

"How's the vomit machine?" the wizard asked cheerfully.

Ben gave him the finger.

"I've never seen that gesture before, but from the look on your face, I'm fairly sure I get the gist." Kural leaned on the railing. "In all seriousness, I do hope the rest of our journey—as short as it is—is less unpleasant."

He nodded vaguely and considered whether or not he could get his vomit over the railing without moving. Probably not, which was unfortunate.

"Only a few more hours," Zaara said encouragingly. She hopped up on the railing.

"Ugh," he said. "Don't do that."

"I swear you're worse than my grandmother when it comes to this stuff." She rolled her eyes. "I'm *fine*."

"One wrong wave and into the soup you'll go," he warned her. Unfortunately, his turn of phrase led him to think about soup—a topic that did his stomach no favors. He uttered a little moan and tipped his head back against the bulkhead.

"He has a point," Kural said. "Besides which, the waves *are* getting higher as the storm moves in."

Ben wasn't watching, but he knew Zaara well enough to know that she rolled her eyes. He tried to calm his stomach through sheer force of will and asked, "Do you think we'll beat the storm into port?" The idea of rain on his face was nice, but the higher waves would, he was sure, more than compensate for the rain.

"It's hard to say for sure," the wizard said. "I'd guess so, but— oh. Hmm."

"What?" He opened his eyes.

A moment later, a crack of thunder made him leap like a deranged squirrel, and rain began to fall.

"You know, I don't think we will beat the storm," Kural said contemplatively.

He would have rolled his eyes except that he was now bent over the side of the ship, throwing up again. The vessel rolled on a high swell and dipped crazily toward the water, something he had still not adjusted to, and he wound his arms around the railing with a yelp.

The protest was full of vomit.

Zaara also yelped—a vomitless one—and scrambled down from the railing. He was glad they wouldn't have to do an aquatic rescue but vaguely disappointed that she hadn't wound up in the cold water as a consequence of her ill-advised actions. If he was honest with himself, he had to admit that her general gracefulness was simply annoying to him given his present predicament of trying to get motor control back.

Was it too much to ask to have *other* people trip and fall once in a while to remind him that he wasn't the only clumsy one?

The boat rocked strongly again, and Ben refocused on the problem at hand. The rain fell more heavily now and darkened the deck. He wrapped his arms more firmly around the railing and listened as sailors banged through the door onto the deck. Several of them scrambled nimbly up the rigging, which he knew from experience made him sick if he watched.

Great. Exactly what he needed for his last few hours on this ship—higher waves and more vomit. If they had to send him inside and out of the fresh air, it would be even worse. The thought made his stomach twist and he opened his mouth instinctively.

It filled with seawater as a wave caught him squarely in the face. Ben yelled and gargled salt water, which did nothing to improve the way his mouth tasted. The wave broke across the deck and his side of the vessel tipped into the air to leave him clinging to the railing and shivering violently.

"Ben!" Kural hurried closer, also holding fast to the railing to keep from slipping. "We have to get you inside!"

"No!" The shout was mostly an expression of dislike. He was already plotting his path to the door. His side of the boat plunged again and precipitated a sickening drop in the pit of his stomach. His back struck the railing squarely and in the next moment, Zaara bolted past him at high speed.

"I'll go first!" she called and raced across the deck like she was sprinting up a hill.

"Zaara!" Ben yelled as the ship tipped again.

She slipped, wind-milled her arms, and barely managed to catch hold of the door. It slammed open, took her with it by its momentum, and banged into the wall to elicit a curse from her.

She hunched her shoulders and hung on as a wave covered her in salty spray, then nodded at him. "Okay, go now!"

"Are you *crazy*?" Staying outside didn't seem like a very good idea, but running across a slippery and wildly tilting deck seemed like a worse one.

"I am not crazy!" she yelled in response. "Ben, you have to run. Start when you're going uphill and try to get yourself into that stairwell."

"I hate this idea!" he shouted and was doused in salt water again a moment later.

"Ben! Go *now*!"

His mind was a blank but his body worked—a welcome change. He unwound his arms from the railing and launched himself toward the door. His boots provided enough purchase to keep him from slipping, thank goodness.

The boat rocked to the other side. His mind flashed through images of him stumbling past Zaara, flipping over the railing, flailing into seawater, and coughing and choking. He didn't know if he could control his body well enough to swim and these were hardly good conditions for it.

He put all his focus on the door and leapt forward.

At the same moment, the vessel tipped again and created the illusion that the doorway had lunged forward to swallow him. Ben—who had been worried he wouldn't make it at all a split second before—now hurtled into the darkness at high speed.

It could have been worse if he'd registered every detail. He was fairly sure his mind turned off during his tumble down the stairs, for which he was glad. When he came to, he rolled one way to fetch up against one wall with a *thump*, then rolled the other way into the opposite wall. It was, he realized, a repetitive cycle over which he had no control.

He decided to not even try to stand—*thump*—while he made a mental inventory of his—*thump*—injuries and tried to wiggle his —*thump*—fingers.

A moment later, a series of exclamations and thuds announced Kural's arrival. He had one glimpse of the wizard, his robe and spread arms making him look like nothing so much as a flying squirrel, before Kural landed smack on top of him.

The man proceeded to join him in his regular journey between the two walls of the corridor.

It was, Ben thought—*thump*—not the most dignified thing —*thump*—he had ever done.

More yelling intruded, a door slammed, and a moment of silence followed—except, of course, for the series of thumps.

The sound of helpless laughter was unmistakable. He looked up to where Zaara held onto the wall railing and almost sobbed with laughter. As he and Kural rolled to the other side of the corridor, she sank onto the stairs, grasped the railing with both arms, and buried her face in her elbow. She made little whooping noises while she watched them.

The wizard gave her an unfriendly look.

"I don't suppose you would consider helping us rather than laughing at us."

This only set her off again, but her laughter turned into a shriek when the ship pitched wildly. Ben made a hawking noise and Kural tried to escape, but his efforts only precipitated another tumble down the hallway in a series of thumps and exclamations.

It took a great deal of effort and a few close calls with Ben's stomach, but the three of them managed to get into their cabin to strap in. He wondered, as his body tensed against the restraints, whether he should be worried. Suddenly, he was very aware of how they had shut themselves inside a tiny capsule.

Every time his body lurched against the straps, he remembered the jerk when the rope had first broken his fall on the rock face—and the sudden slackness, paired with Mike's yell, that told him it hadn't been enough to *truly* catch him.

He closed his eyes and realized he was praying.

Mutters caught his attention and he opened his eyes as Zaara and Kural reached out to clasp their hands together. At first, he thought they were also praying. Then he saw the faint shimmer of magic in the air and realized they were working on the storm.

Ben lost track of how many times the pitch and roll of the ship threw him against the restraints, and it wasn't long before his stomach betrayed him beyond his ability to control it. Through it all, however, his companions' focus never wavered.

Slowly and gradually, the waves quieted.

"You stopped the storm," he whispered when Zaara opened her eyes.

She responded with a tired shake of her head. "We only hurried us through it—unwinding a storm is too much for any two wizards to do. Kural will maintain our speed and I'll go tell the captain." She smiled with exhaustion. "So the good news is that you'll get off this boat sooner than you thought."

His thumbs-up was accompanied by a sickly gurgle.

CHAPTER THREE

"Okay," Nick said as Jamie lay back in the pod. "You've done this before so you know the drill. Watch my finger and count back from ten." He began to move his finger from one side to the other so the boy had to track the movement.

"Ten," Jamie said. He swallowed, terrified of the idea of the lid closing over him. He loved the game but he was also claustrophobic and this fear haunted him every time he lay on the pod bed.

"Keep counting," the engineer said.

"Right." He was very sure the drugs were taking hold. "Nine, eight, seven..."

He blinked and opened his eyes to blue sky. His mind adjusted and took in more detail, and he realized that he lay on a bed of soft grass, listened to the chirp of insects, and heard the wind in the grass.

"Oof." He sat quickly. "Prima?"

"I'm here. Welcome back."

"Thank you." He stood and looked at his clothes. "I see I've retained my slightly less awful clothing."

"Yes, and I encourage you to continue in that direction."

"First things first," Jamie said. "Where is Taigan?"

"She's on her way to the edge of the forest. You'll want to meet her there."

He set off so hastily that he forgot to check which direction the forest was in and had to reverse course a moment later. The AI snickered at that but didn't give voice to any snubs, which suited him fine.

The land through which he traveled was familiar to him, with pink grass and glowing flowers, but he was certain the forest hadn't been there last time. He was sure he would remember trees like those—redwoods that reminded him of childhood trips to California.

His heart thudded so loudly that he could hear it in his ears, and its tempo only increased as he scanned the tree line. Every glimpse of movement made his heart leap. He would see her soon, round-faced and skinny, hopping over tree roots.

Soon.

Taigan scrambled onto a massive tree root and walked along it with her arms out for balance. She began to get out of breath and she savored the feel of sweat running down her back. While she had never liked humidity or getting sweaty when she was on Earth, the reminder of her as a person with a body was something she loved.

She couldn't get over how wonderful it was to do something as mundane as scratching her nose. The little details made all the difference, she thought as she rubbed her back and enjoyed the feeling of cloth over sweat-slick skin.

The edge of the forest grew closer. She had walked all morning and the trees were definitely getting smaller. Sometimes, if she found the right angle, she could even see out into what was beyond—a meadow that looked almost pink.

As if inviting her, a breeze lifted her hair. She could smell flowers. This wind had come from the plains, not from the trees.

The girl began to run. She loved running and always had. It was one of the best ways to lose herself and she was fast too, but with her dropping out of school so frequently, none of the coaches had wanted to take a chance on her not being there for a big meet.

Every time she ran, she told herself that if she could only run fast enough, she would fix it all. If she ran fast enough, she would ace that test—or get what she wanted for her birthday, or the guy she liked would give her a call. It didn't always work but she believed in it anyway.

If she ran fast enough, she would wake up.

Taigan tucked her arms against her skinny body and focused everything she had on the glimpses of pink through the trees. She hurdled tree roots and leapt over dips in the ground as she pushed herself to go faster. She could always go faster. Her body never failed her—not in this.

If she ran fast enough, she would wake up.

Sweat trickled down the side of her neck and her breath came rapidly. She wanted to laugh and scream with how happy she was. Everything was working, she was home in this body, and she *existed*. And if she existed, she could wake up.

The grass came ever closer.

"Jamie is waiting for you," Prima told her, and Taigan let her legs push her to greater speed.

Jamie—who could read her thoughts, who annoyed her more than anyone else in the world, but who she could never live without. He had never told her how desperately alone he felt when his twin was in a coma, but she had found his journal, read it, and cried herself to sleep for three nights afterward.

He would know she was still alive.

She burst out of the trees and into the grass. "Jamie! Jamie!" She laughed as she spun in search of him. "Jamie! I'm here." She rested her hands on top of her head and tipped her head back to breathe. "Jamie?" she called, her eyes still closed. "Prima—am I in the wrong place?"

The long moment of silence became uncomfortable.

"Prima?" Taigan felt the first flicker of unease. If Prima was offline, it meant—

Well, she didn't know what it meant, but it couldn't be *good*.

"Prima, are you still here?"

"I'm still here."

"Thank crap for that. Where's Jamie?"

Another pause followed.

"He's here," the AI said finally. *"He's standing in front of you and you're both here. He doesn't see you, though, and you don't see him. I..."* She had been worried before that she'd hurt Taigan's feelings. But this worry was different. *"I don't understand,"* she finished finally.

"Prima?" Jamie turned in place. "Do you have any idea when she'll get here?"

It wasn't Prima's fault, he reminded himself. He had worked himself up in his head. The image he'd held onto was that he would see her as she burst out of the trees and they'd share the particular smile they had—one that said, "You know me better than anyone else."

It drove Emilia nuts.

He knew no one was to blame for him arriving at the forest too early so he had to stand around and kick dirt awkwardly. It merely felt like a letdown, that was all.

Prima didn't answer for a moment. When she did speak, her voice was as gentle as he'd ever heard it.

"Jamie, I'm sorry."

"What?" Panic spiked. "What? Prima, what *happened?*" Something had happened to Taigan. A heart attack, an accident, the coma had—no, no, no. "She's—" He wanted to throw up. He'd pushed to have her put into this game, he'd yelled at his parents and they'd done it, and he'd killed her. Thanks to his obstinacy, he'd killed his sister and it should have been him.

"Jamie! What's wrong?"

"What's wrong? It's all my fault, that's what's wrong. I killed her!"

What? The AI sounded astonished—then horrified. *"Is that what you thought was going on? That she was dead?"*

He stopped in his tracks. "She's…not?"

"No!"

"Why would you say you were sorry like that?" He shrieked the words at the sky.

"Because I was sorry. Something seems to be glitching and you're both here but you can't see each other. Something isn't working and the game is me, so it's my fault. I said I was sorry because I was sorry." She sounded almost panicked. *"How did you get her being dead out of that?"*

"Oh, my God." Jamie sank onto the ground. His heart pounded and he felt dizzy.

He also still wanted to hurl.

"Oh, my God," he muttered again. "Holy shit. Prima, never scare me like that again. Never, never, never. Oh, my God."

"I still don't understand," she said plaintively.

"Okay…maybe don't introduce bad news that way again." Laughter bubbled in his chest. It wasn't dignified laughter, much more on the hysterical end of the spectrum. "Holy shit. Holy *shit*. Holy shit."

She was alive. He didn't care that he couldn't see her.

They could work the rest of it out. As long as she was alive, there was hope.

He had thought his sister was *dead*. Prima could not understand that at all. She would need to comb through linguistics databases again.

Maybe another time, however, because right now, she needed to understand why the two of them couldn't see each other. They were both there, after all—in fact, in a feat that was statistically improbable, they had emerged at almost exactly the same place.

She was given to understand that, where twins were concerned, there was a considerable number of coincidences. The AI filed this away to run simulations on it later.

They simply couldn't *see* each other. Now that was a pickle as DuBois would say. She liked how he talked. He was the one out of the crew who she understood the best.

Carefully, she studied the output that told her about each of them. She had access to a feed on heart rate and blood pressure—both elevated in each of the twins right now—internal temperature, CO2 levels, hormone levels, and an active brain scan.

Taigan's brain looked different than Jamie's, of course, but it always did. It was closer to something she recognized as a waking state, but it wasn't all the way there.

Ah. Maybe that was it.

Prima studied the way the two of them manifested in her code. Jamie was like Justin or Ben—smooth around the edges. Taigan was…spikier. Her edges wavered like static. She existed differently as if she were a TV out of tune.

While she watched, the girl kicked the ground. She wasn't annoyed, she could see, merely bored and she glanced at the little puff of dust with vague interest.

And so did Jamie.

"Can you see the dust?" the AI asked him.

"Yes, what *was* that?" A second later, he seemed to realize what was going on. "That was her?" He stretched his hands out and edged forward as if he were in a dark room.

Unfortunately, he walked right through her.

This was most certainly a pickle. Prima would have shaken her head if she had one. As it was, she made a small *hmmm* noise in her circuits.

"You can't see each other," she reported to both of them, *"but you can see the effect the other makes on the world. Taigan, when you kicked the ground, Jamie saw the puff of dirt."*

"He did?" The girl looked up, her eyes wide. She stamped her foot on the ground again.

Jamie responded with a crazed laugh and did the same. It rapidly turned into a vague type of fight as they kicked dust in the other's direction—although the dust that coated Taigan's face in her part of the world floated through her in Jamie's.

It didn't take them long, either, to realize that they could do more than simply throw dust. Taigan knelt to drag her finger through the dirt: *I MISS YOU*, she spelled.

He uttered a laugh that sounded more than half like a sob. He knelt to clear another patch of ground. *I MISS YOU TOO.*

She hesitated. *THANK YOU FOR COMING TO GET ME.*

I DIDN'T DO A VERY GOOD JOB OF IT, DID I?

WE'RE BOTH HERE. Her answer was immediate. *I'M NOT ALONE. THANK YOU.* Tears welled in her eyes. *WE'LL FIGURE IT OUT. RIGHT?*

WE'LL FIGURE IT OUT, he wrote at once. *I WON'T LEAVE HERE WITHOUT YOU.*

Quietly and carefully, Taigan reached out in her brother's direction. She left her palm hovering in the air. He couldn't see her but he stretched his hand out as well. They passed through each other, the spacing not quite right.

But they knew. Prima was sure of it. They knew what the other was doing.

CHAPTER FOUR

When the ship limped into port at Heffog that evening, no one on board looked particularly reputable or vaguely neat. Kural and Ben were both bruised to hell and back, as were many of the sailors. Most of the group were still damp, with a tiny crust of salt crystals in eyebrows and beards.

Even Zaara, who managed to be elegant at the worst of times, looked like she simply wanted to sink into the ground and hide.

After making sure all their possessions had been unloaded, the wizard cast a critical look at his companions and summoned a carriage with a whistle. "A meal and sleep first," he said. His tone left no room for argument.

She didn't do anything other than nod, which did more to convince Ben of her exhaustion than anything else. Every once in a while, however, she would giggle and he *knew* she pictured him and Kural rolling across the ship's floor.

He glowered and nursed his bruises.

The carriage they had was less of an elegant conveyance on sprung wheels and more of a converted farm wagon with pieces of hay and cabbage still on the floor. He had initially been too tired to care about anything other than his lack of seasickness but was now jostled so painfully that he could not get comfortable at any point during the journey.

Heffog was nothing like the fae lands. Everything there had been beautiful and sleek, in soft colors or brilliant crystal, clean and scented with flowers. The city was filthy. Instead of empty corridors, streets were filled with so many people that the cart barely had room to get through. The buildings near the docks were all jumbled together. Dingy houses and shops made of plaster and exposed beams stood wall to wall with leaning shanties with roofs scraped together from tarps and pieces of stone and pottery.

Not only that, it smelled of seawater, both old and new fish, and a great number of things he did not want to know about. The resulting mix was unique.

They arrived at the inn after what seemed to be an interminable journey. Now freed from seasickness, Ben's stomach grumbled loudly—something that didn't relate well to the particular set of smells he encountered.

The driver helped them haul their trunks into the inn, where the proprietor informed them that there was only one room left with one bed. Kural haggled a lower price with remarkable skill, clearly unimpressed and still slightly and unsettlingly blue-skinned, and their trunks were brought up.

Inside the inn, things smelled marginally better, the worst offenders being stale beer and the odor of fish that seemed to permeate everywhere in this godforsaken town. At a glance, Ben saw humans and dwarves in abundance but no orcs or fae. Or elves, come to think of it.

"Keep your head down," the wizard advised him in low tones.

"What? Someone will shank me if I look around?" He was more intrigued than anything else.

"No," the man said, his tone one of long-suffering. "They'll try to sell you things."

"That's easy enough to manage. I don't have any money."

"You'd think it would be so simple, wouldn't you?" Kural asked in dire tones.

Ben looked at Zaara, who only shrugged. She didn't appear to be willing to interrupt her eating with conversation. Spiced beans and greens had been served with a platter of flatbreads instead of utensils, and she had wasted no time in using the flatbreads to make little packets of stew, which she popped cheerfully in her mouth.

Initially dubious of the whole concept, he came around quickly when he realized the stew was hearty and savory, set off nicely by both the mild taste of the flatbread and the slight cut of the beer. He felt like he hadn't eaten in days—which, given the amount of food that had successfully stayed in his stomach during the journey, was probably true.

They ceded their table to one of the clusters of merchants who stood around drinking and headed upstairs to the room. It was small, with a bed that could only *possibly* fit one of them. He suspected it had been made with a dwarf in mind.

"Zaara gets the bed," Kural said. "She's the shortest. Ben, help me spread the bedrolls."

"I don't suppose there's any chance of a bath," she said longingly.

"There are public baths. Well, there were the last time I was here." The wizard scratched his chin. "That was over a century ago, though, so I couldn't tell you. This also used to be the heart of the fish market. Things change." He yawned widely. "Either way, it's time to get some rest."

Ben also wanted a shower, but the bedroll seemed to call his name fairly loudly. It couldn't hurt to rest for a few minutes, he decided. He'd resolve the shower or bath situation after that.

He woke well over twelve hours later. When he opened his eyes, it was to faint sunlight creeping in behind the shutters. After a moment, he realized that what he had thought was a chainsaw battle outside was, in fact, Zaara and Kural competing to see who could snore the loudest.

As far as he was concerned, both were winning. The loser was anyone in a hundred-yard radius.

With a scowl, he remained where he was and wiggled his fingers and feet until they woke up. He was hungry but still too tired and bruised to want to move.

After a brief breakfast—people in Heffog apparently did not believe in that particular meal—Zaara and Kural headed off to find a conveyance to Insea and left him with strict instructions to not get into trouble.

Ben had heard that often in his life, and he wasn't about to start listening now.

He pushed into the crush of the streets. The city was as crowded as it had been the day before, and he was startled to see what looked like obscenely rich people mingling with the poor and the merchants. Fishmongers called prices to people in gold brocade, who answered as often as those in burlap.

A surprising number of children were present—many stood beside their parents at market stalls, some babies slept in slings on people's backs or were carried on their shoulders, and still more darted underfoot.

What surprised him most was how much he was enjoying himself. Ben had always been someone who enjoyed remote, quiet places. He enjoyed beautiful views and silent mornings, but something about the impersonal crush made him feel almost as free there as he had ever been in the mountains. Everywhere he looked, he caught another flash of color, a smile, a laugh, a new smell, or a beautiful piece of art.

He shoved his hands into his pockets and forged through the crowd. In all honesty, he wasn't sure where he was going—only that it gradually sloped uphill and away from the piers. Little stalls or blankets on the ground slowly gave way to storefronts with painted wooden signs, and the people began to thin. The streets were only marginally less dirty, but from the painted touches on the buildings to the general level of clothing, he could tell that he was in a classier area.

In addition, he drew a fair number of dirty looks too, which he conceded he deserved, all things considered. He was a strange man crusted in salt who didn't quite walk correctly.

A child brushed past him and raced away with a quick call of, "Sorry!" over his shoulder.

Ben hardly had time to process that before a woman pounced. She had been leaning in a shop door, so quiet and unassuming that he hadn't noticed her, but she lunged out of the aperture with surprising speed and grasped a handful of the child's shirt. The young one yelped and scrabbled at her hand.

"Give the man his purse," she instructed. She hauled the child to where he stood with his mouth open.

"I don't think he—" He patted his pockets, then gaped again. The woman was completely correct. What little money he had was gone. "Huh."

"I didn't take it," the child protested. He glared at the woman. "Check my pockets."

"I could," she said and sounded bored. Her skin held a faintly purplish hue, although she didn't look entirely like an elf, and her hair was night-black. She leaned closer to the child and smiled to reveal a large number of teeth. "*Or* I could do *this* until you give him the purse." Her other hand snaked out and twisted his ear.

"Stop it!" Ben protested as the child yelped and tried to free himself.

"It's fine," she said cheerfully. She hung on as her captive sank to his knees. "It won't harm him."

"But you're *hurting* him," he said, not sure what else to say.

"Mm-hmm...that's the point." She tilted her head to the side and must have increased the pressure in her hands because the child shrieked and threw the purse into the air. She caught it with a grim smile, handed it to Ben, and released the culprit. "I don't want to see you pickpocketing my customers again," she told him.

The boy ran off, holding his ear.

"Do you honestly think that will stop him from stealing?" he asked skeptically.

"Who said anything about him not stealing?" the woman asked quizzically. "I told him I didn't want to *see* him doing it."

He opened his mouth but closed it with a snap.

Her mouth twitched. "You're a strange one. Where are you from?"

"Colorado," he said wryly. "It's very far away."

"It must be." Her eyebrows quirked. "Journey well, stranger."

"Why…" He looked around quickly and realized there weren't many people there. "Why did you help me?"

She looked uneasy at that—enough so that he was intrigued. After a slight hesitation, she raised one shoulder in a studied gesture of indifference and said carelessly, "You looked helpless. I couldn't simply let him prey on the weak." As if to assure him that she wasn't soft, she added, "Not to mention that his form was terrible and he needed a lesson."

Ben didn't know what to say to that, but he began to have a hunch about who she was. Before he stopped to consider that this might be a terrible question, he took a hasty breath and asked, "So…do you run this part of town?"

Thankfully, she threw her head back and laughed. It was genuine and full of warmth that surprised him given the black hair, cool skin, and acerbic advice.

"Do you think I run a protection racket?" she asked when she stopped chuckling. "Take fees from all the shops, swagger in and make nice-sounding threats? Dump a few bodies in the bay when I get screwed over?"

The ease with which she spoke of it was chilling, but there was no mistaking her derision for that way of life and he wanted to know more. "Okay, I was clearly wrong." He folded his arms and smiled at her. "Enlighten me."

"Look at you, asking for a king's ransom worth of information so casually." She smiled, leaned in the doorway, and mirrored his folded arms. "Genuine curiosity, though, unless I miss my guess. I have no interest in threatening my neighbors or having little territorial spats with gangs. It's hardly conducive to a pleasant existence, for one thing. It's also tiring."

"Does this mean you once *tried* to be a crime boss?"

"Again with the questions." She seemed to be enjoying herself. "Theft is the fuel that powers this city, traveler. It is a shadow on every transaction at the market, on every good that crosses your palm, and every coin you spend. In the end, it unbalances the world...and I re-balance it."

"Eh?"

"I mean," she said, amused, "that gold is wrung out of the bodies of the poor while their sweat and blood trickles through the strata and the shadows and lies...and I take back what was stolen."

"Robin Hood," Ben said, understanding at last.

"Hmm?"

"Steal from the rich, give to the poor?"

"Ah. Close enough." She shrugged.

"Doesn't that seem somewhat roundabout?" he asked quizzically. "Shouldn't you change the whole system?"

She stared at him. "Sure. I think I have a few spare minutes before my dinner—or do you think we should set aside a whole evening?"

"Point taken," he said and grinned. "So...is this attacking caravans in the night with a whole group of mercenaries, or pickpocketing merchants who wander past you, or what?"

"Always with the questions. Do you ever stop asking them?"

"Speaking from experience," Kural said, "no."

Ben jerked around to focus on his two companions. "Where did you two come from?"

"From a caravan leader's shop," Zaara said. "How did *you* wind up making the acquaintance of the best thief in three cities?"

The woman scoffed. "Three? Make it the world."

Zaara rolled her eyes.

"Picking pockets, then?" Ben asked.

"Sometimes. For fun." She shrugged. "But I usually go after larger prizes. It means more time and effort and a great deal more gain."

"Elantria helped Kural when he was first defeated by Sephith," Zaara explained. "She found him the artifacts that helped him recover some portion of his powers as well as transform and be able to venture safely toward East Newbrook again."

"Ancient history," the wizard said shortly as Elantria said, "Less details, if you please."

"You know," Prima commented in his head, *"you're doing fairly well on gross motor control. Perhaps it's time to switch your focus to fine motor skills."*

His eyebrows raised in surprise. Was she suggesting what he thought she was?

Hmm.

Before he could stop himself by thinking too hard about it, he blurted the question. "Would you have any interest in taking on an apprentice?"

His friends both gaped. The woman stared at him for a moment. Her eyes scanned him intently, a deep enough scrutiny that he blushed.

"Why?" she asked finally.

"I like learning things," Ben said promptly and Zaara put her face in one hand.

"Done," the other woman said.

Zaara's head jerked up. "Wait, really?"

"Really." Elantria smiled at him. "A strange man from what sounds like a strange homeland—and he has a pair of stones on him to boot. I like that."

CHAPTER FIVE

Ben woke early the next morning to see his two companions off with their caravan. It turned out that trade caravans between Heffog and Insea were accustomed to taking passengers as extra funding for the trip, so the two of them had been able to secure places without much trouble.

They had intended to take another ship to Insea, but after the storm, neither of them wanted to go back on the open water.

Zaara yawned and clutched a wooden mug of tea as she embraced Ben with one arm. "This is your last chance," she said through her yawns. "Are you sure you don't want to come with us? They'll grumble but that's simply out of principle. They'd be happy to have you."

"She's right, you know." Kural nodded at him. "Conservatively, about forty percent of a leader's time is spent doing performative grumbling."

He smiled at the two of them. Only a couple of weeks before, he had loathed the man, but it turned out the wizard was merely an acquired taste. Zaara, meanwhile, was someone he could make neither head nor tail of. Just when he thought he had a grasp on who she was, she showed another side.

For one thing, he didn't think she was entirely convinced that she wanted to spend a centuries-long life alone. He would have said something but he suspected that wouldn't be taken well.

Now, he shook his head firmly. "I want to stay here," he said. It was something he had repeated several times over the past sixteen hours or so, mostly because they constantly repeated the question.

"And learn to be a master thief?" Zaara asked skeptically.

"You don't have to be obvious about your lack of faith, you know."

"First, I can't use facts and now, I'm not supposed to be honest? What conversational gambits do I have left?"

"You know very well I wasn't talking to you," he mumbled so the others wouldn't hear.

"It seems like such a big change," Zaara said, having sleepily missed his argument with Prima. "We met two weeks ago and you weren't willing to even consider violence because it so compromised your ethics. Now, you're heaving caution to the winds and training for a life of crime? It honestly seems like too much of a stretch."

He had to admit she had a point and gnawed at his lip while he considered his choice. His decision had been impulsive, based on Prima's mention of fine motor control. On that front, he was honest with himself. But he couldn't tell Zaara that, obviously, and he was also able to admit to himself that he stayed for reasons he didn't entirely understand.

"I'm staying to learn how to do these things," he said. "I don't necessarily intend to use them."

"You could cut yourself on that knife-edge," she said cheerfully. "So handle it carefully."

Ben was still laughing as the caravan set out. His friends would return to Insea to update their mysterious leaders on their equally mysterious and vital peace missions. No matter how many drinks he bought them, they still hadn't told him exactly what the problem was.

Which didn't matter, he decided. They both seemed to be doing the best they could for the world, and for all he knew, their seemingly opposed natures—Zaara the young idealist and Kural the world-weary pragmatist—would help them achieve more together than they ever could apart.

When the caravan moved out of sight and he refocused, it occurred to him that he was completely alone in a strange city without much money or a place to stay.

And he also didn't know how to get in touch with Elantria. He'd wandered aimlessly the day before and wasn't sure where he'd been. What if he couldn't find her again—or if she had been joking about training him as an apprentice?

"I've made a huge mistake," he said to Prima.

"You'll have to be more specific."

He glowered at the sky. "I should have gone with Zaara and Kural."

"So why aren't you running after the caravan right now?"

"I...okay, that's a good question."

"I thought so." She paused and he simply waited. *"Do you intend to answer it?"* she demanded.

"I thought it was rhetorical."

"No, I wanted the answer. It has been a rough few days when it comes to communication with people, I'll tell you that. The way you use language is..."

"More an art than a science," he suggested smartly.

"I wanted to say 'completely fucking bonkers,' but sure, put a good spin on it if you want."

Ben was still snickering when a woman behind him asked, "Who are you talking to?"

He leapt in alarm and stifled a shout. When he turned, Elantria studied him with her eyes narrowed. If she hadn't already been regretting her choice to help him, he was fairly certain she did now.

Carefully, he weighed his options, considered what he knew of the world, and said finally, "I'm possessed by a demon."

"What the fuck did you call me?"

The woman stared at him before she walked up to him, pried one of his eyelids up, and examined it. She opened his jaws forcibly, pulled his tongue forward, and made a thorough inventory of his teeth. A few more tests followed, each seemingly meaningless from his perspective.

"Whatever's in you," she said finally, "it's not a demon."

"That was more a turn of phrase I had chosen. I can hear a very powerful being who likes to make fun of me."

Elantria considered this. "Do you think it will help or hinder your ability to be a thief?" she asked finally.

"You have a very one-track mind, don't you?"

"It's what makes me good at what I do." She folded her arms and looked at him. "So?"

"She'll probably make me better at it," he said.

"Not until you apologize for calling me a demon, I won't."

"Good," his companion said. As an afterthought, she added, "And don't tell anyone else you have a demon in your head. There's a whole gang of demon-killers in the city and they'd gut you before asking questions."

Ben could feel Prima's smugness radiated at him. He sighed and nodded.

"For your first assignment," Elantria told him, "you have to find out who the most successful merchant in the Sunset Market is." She smiled at him, took a running leap to jump up onto the wall, and began to scale it.

"Wait!" he called after her. "Where is the Sunset Market? How do you define most successful?"

She gave him a grin as she reached the roof but didn't answer and simply ran lightly across the tiles. He blew his breath out in annoyance and paused to think.

Well, he knew one thing he had to do first, at any rate. "Prima? I'm sorry for calling you a demon."

Sulky silence was his only answer.

"You're more powerful than a human," he explained, "and you like to play tricks on us. That's either a demon or a fairy, and I recently met some fairies. You're clearly not one of those."

"Hmmm."

"They don't know what computers are here so how was I supposed to explain AI?"

"Golems are a thing, you know." She sounded mollified, however. *"Very well, let's get to it."*

"Good. Where am I going?"

"I'm not doing everything for you, you know."

Ben threw his hands up and walked through the gates. On the other side stood two soldiers who had clearly heard some of his conversations and who looked around for a companion. He tried to hasten out of sight before they realized there wasn't one but also to not walk so quickly that he looked like he had committed a crime.

After considering his options, he decided to start by going downhill. This led to the bay, and he had seen a market there the day before. That might be the Sunset Market for all he knew.

He took notice of all the small details today. Some of the buildings were as lovingly made and magically maintained as the *Wind Dancer* and looked untouched by time. Generally, these were surrounded by more common types of mansions made of stone or plaster, with turrets and balconies. The city also seemed to be a mishmash of rich and poor, however, with beggars on even the most upper-class corners and shacks built in the alleys between the homes.

After a while, he glanced at the sun. He had learned how to

tell both time and direction from the sun when he was in the Boy Scouts and that simple trick had served him well.

In the early-morning light, it also gave him an idea. Zaara and Kural had left the city via a road that wound north. He took a moment to center himself, then turned west. The Sunset Market. Maybe it would be on the western side of the city.

He passed through neighborhoods that were dingy and some that were clean. Both private guards and city officers watched him from under wide-brimmed hats. A few people called out to him, most with words he had never heard before. Sometimes, he guessed from their wares that they were selling food of some kind.

Occasionally—as with the man who held a carved amulet out that made his skin crawl—it seemed that they sold something more occult in nature.

More than once, he thought he saw groups of people huddled in the shadows, some with iron collars or manacles.

"Prima," he murmured. "What am I seeing?"

"*I think you know.*"

"I…why are they here? Why put slavery in this world?"

"*Slavery is all around you,*" she said. Although her words sounded grandiose, she seemed quite serious. "*In this world, it is simply in front of your eyes.*"

Ben swallowed and hurried on with his head down. He tried so hard not to notice anything that he didn't see the Sunset Market until he was almost past it.

It was at once the most intriguing and most depressing place he had ever seen. This wasn't simply because it existed on the southern side of the city. It was that it was composed of things others hadn't been able to sell. Wilted cabbages and battered fruit smelled like they were on the edge of rot. Scraps of cloth were tied together into bales and any number of stalls boasted broken odds and ends.

He walked through for a few minutes before he remembered why he was there and immediately realized that he had no idea where to begin.

With no real plan, he began to look at the items he walked past. Was it the fruit and vegetable vendors, he wondered? Surely there would always be a market for food, no matter how close it was to being spoiled. Or perhaps the cloth, which had less of a time limitation?

At the corner of the market, he noticed a merchant with wares that glittered. He drifted closer and tried not to get caught looking directly at the stall. Soon, he was close enough to identify glittering rings and jewels. Many of them were probably fake but he guessed that some were real—and liberated creatively from their prior owners.

This, surely, must be the most successful merchant.

He knew from the silence behind him that Elantria was there. She came to stand next to him.

"Have you made your guess?" she asked.

Ben was about to open his mouth to speak when something in her manner stopped him. It was too easy. It seemed far too obvious. He turned and looked at the stalls. Was it the most customers or the most valuable wares?

The woman was smiling when he looked at her. She sighed—not one of disappointment but one of acceptance—and nodded toward the edge of the market. At first, he didn't understand what she was saying. The woman she had indicated was old and bent, dressed in rags, and sold broken pieces of pottery. She surely could not be the most successful merchant.

Then, he saw the building. Somehow, even in a fantasy world, banks still looked like banks.

"Those who hold and change the money," Elantria said, "accrue it. Each of these vendors pays a fee to the people who surround this market so they won't be driven out. In turn, they can get an advance on their sales—for interest, of course. Some of the prime positions are owned and sold by the oldest names in the city. You looked at the market, apprentice, not at the shadow in which it sat."

CHAPTER SIX

Ben woke the next morning with every muscle in his back and shoulders cramped. Elantria had offered him a place to sleep and had assured him it was safe.

It was on a small balcony with no bed.

He had a bedroll and a small pack, courtesy of the fae king, but it made very little difference to a hard floor. She had shown it to him with a twinkle in her eye that suggested she was waiting for him to protest, and he hadn't wanted to give her the satisfaction.

If she tried to pull some crap where he had to do menial chores to learn various techniques, he was out.

A moment later, another rock struck him and he realized why he had woken up. He turned, winced in pain, and looked at the floor.

"Good morning," Elantria said. "You certainly slept in."

"I'm recovering from—you know what? Never mind." He stood and looked into the courtyard. "Is it training time? Is there breakfast?"

"There *is* breakfast, and the sooner you learn your first skill, the sooner you can have it." She pointed to the wall. "Climb down."

"I would, but—"

"But nothing."

He bit back an angry retort and also decided not to dwell on the fact that things like this were exactly why he had chosen to stay there. Kural and Zaara had been supportive, caring, and eager to pull chairs out for him and carry his trunk. From the first conversation with Elantria, he'd known she wouldn't do any of those things.

She would push him and didn't care at all about any protests he might have.

"*Move.*"

Right. He studied the wall with a critical eye. There was an easy path but a few of the holds were plaster and he had no idea if they would crumble under his fingertips. The thought of that brought to mind a very unpleasant memory of climbing on a sandstone formation. Up until recently, Ben would have classified that as his worst climbing memory, but the accident had blown it out of the water.

Thinking about the fall made his heart race. He swallowed convulsively and threw one leg over the balcony, straddled it for a moment, and felt the creak of the old posts. That was sufficient to make him decide not to waste any more time.

After all, everyone said that when you had a fall, you couldn't recover until you climbed again. And nothing could *happen* to him there, right?

"*Are you sure this is a good idea?*"

"Not now," he muttered and gritted his teeth.

The building was three stories high and his balcony was on the second. Irregular bricks and blocks of stone had been piled together haphazardly and plastered over. The weather had worn and battered the plaster over the years to leave holds that were both tempting and dangerous.

Ben eased out onto the wall and let his breath out slowly. Every muscle in his body was shaking.

Now, he merely had to move his foot. He had located a promising rock only a short distance below his initial foothold, and it was best to start small.

All had to do was move his foot.

It's no big deal. Move your foot and you're there.

He began to hyperventilate and clung to the wall. No matter how hard he held on, he could feel himself hurtle down and the jerk as the rope went taught and his body flopped like a ragdoll.

The sound of crumbling plaster jerked him out of his reverie. He reacted on instinct, grasped another handhold, and braced himself.

At least he still remembered how to do some things. That was good.

With adrenaline-fueled caution, he inched down the wall in fits and starts. Every time his body moved gracefully, the movement would end slightly in the wrong place or his arms would move out of time with his legs. By the time he reached the bottom, he was coated with sweat and his forearms and fingers ached. It was such a rookie mistake to hold on too tightly with his hands, but all the confidence had been stripped out of him.

He turned to meet Elantria's eyes and waited for the derision.

"I can see it now," she said softly. "You were injured, weren't you? I noticed a strange way of moving yesterday, but I didn't see..." She frowned. "*Where* were you injured?"

Ben thought hard about what to tell her. Would she understand?

"I fell," he said. His voice shook and he hated that. "Badly. I hit my head."

The instinctive concern in her expression came as a surprise and encouraged him to continue.

"Everything seems to be mostly fine," he said. "But I had to relearn...everything...about how to move." He stretched one hand out —which shook visibly, dammit—and stared at the fingers. "Two weeks ago, I couldn't walk and I couldn't eat. Now, I look normal, or close to it."

"Close to it." She didn't sugarcoat things.

"Close to it," he echoed.

She stared at him for a moment. "Well, we won't start you on pick-pocketing, then."

"You planned to teach me pick-pocketing before breakfast?" he demanded. "A nice round of pick-pocketing, then go out to eat?" He realized the truth a moment later. "I would have had to steal my breakfast, wouldn't I?"

"Yep," said Elantria with a ready grin. "Don't worry, I'd never bring you anywhere in this neighborhood—we'd go somewhere posh and where they wouldn't miss a few extra pastries."

"Right, the places with the private guards."

"A brisk run before a meal readies the palate."

Ben couldn't help himself and started to laugh. "This is ridiculous. I can't be a thief."

"Why not? Did your dear old dad want you to be..." She looked speculatively at him. "Something froufy, that's for sure. Clerk?"

"I trained as a chemist," Ben said. When she stared blankly at him, he sighed. "An...alchemist?"

"Oh." She looked at him with more appreciation. "Oh, that's very interesting. Then how did you learn to climb walls? You weren't very coordinated but you clearly knew some tricks."

"I climbed rock faces near my home."

"Good gods." She looked impressed. "Not entirely froufy, then. All right, stay here and I'll be back soon."

He sighed and began some basic stretches. When he had camped or worked outdoors, he had stretched often, simply because there often wasn't anything else to do. What he hadn't realized at the time, being in possession of ample strength and balance, was that stretching used both.

Focused, he moved through the actions and was upside down when the smell of eggs reached his nose and broke his concentration. He fell sideways with a grunt and a muttered expletive and hauled himself up hastily. Elantria waited with two parcels folded in pastry. She handed him one about the size of his palm and opened her mouth to say something when he popped it into his mouth whole.

A moment later, his body went rigid and he danced around the courtyard while he tried to suck quick breaths into his mouth to cool the molten eggs, cheese, and vegetables.

"That's what I wanted to warn you about," she said.

"Iffa hopocka probbem."

"I beg your pardon?"

Ben swallowed his food and winced. It was probably better than keeping it in his mouth but it burned all the way down. "It's the hot pocket problem. Never mind, you won't understand. Ow. Well, that was a breakfast experience."

"And there's another one," Elantria said. "You'll get it after you successfully open that door—which, given that it will give the food time to cool, is good." She tossed him a set of tools wrapped in a piece of leather. "Give it a go, Colorado boy."

"You remembered where I grew up." He was impressed.

"Yes, I looked for it on many maps. I didn't see it." She looked annoyed. "And then the library guards did their rounds and I had to leave."

"Where were the maps?"

"In the palace." She looked at him like he was crazy. "Who *else* has maps?"

He knew better than to find an answer to that. Instead, he unwrapped the tools and moved to the door, which he confirmed was locked before he sat on the ground. He stared at the array of tools and tried to think about what to do.

"To be clear, you want me to accomplish this all on my own?"

"I'd like to watch you try." She shrugged. "It's stupid to not use all of the resources you have available, but you also won't have someone around to ask questions of all the time. Getting the balance is tricky."

"Are there any tips on learning it?" Ben asked. He inserted one of the picks—long and straight—into the keyhole and jiggled it around.

"Not really. You merely keep learning every time you fuck up."

The urge to roll his eyes was strong but he ignored it and wiggled the pick from side to side. He could feel something on the right side. If he wiggled the pick under it—no, over it? He tried to picture how a key would turn in his head. Two tumblers, likely, would have to move.

Clockwise. He briefly considered trying to push them both down with the same tool and decided to add another pick into the mix. Of course, he had meant to ask questions while he did this but he didn't have enough focus for that. He leaned his head forward and tried to do it by feel.

The fact that he was able to do this at all was surprising. He paused.

That realization cost him most of his fledgling motor control. The rest of the lockpicking experience was composed of ten percent skill and forty-five percent each to swearing and sheer stubbornness. More times than he could count, he knocked one of the two picks out of place with the other one.

When he finally positioned them both and the door clicked open, he was too frustrated to even celebrate. He simply dropped the tools and turned to sit with his back against the wall.

Elantria waited for a few moments before she tired of his self-pity. "Pick the tools up. They'll rust."

Ben didn't look at her. It was also difficult to slide each tool into its place, and every tiny challenge annoyed the hell out of him. When it was finally done and the leather rolled and the cord around it even tied in a knot, he sighed. His hands were cramping.

Seriously, he hated this.

"Pick-pocketing would *most certainly* have been the wrong choice," Elantria said. She came to take the tools and give him the other pastry.

His mouth was burned but the food smelled good and his stomach rumbled. He took it and nibbled a corner off so the steam could escape, then ate it in quick, tiny bites.

If he kept eating like this, he would get much thinner. He sighed and rubbed his face.

"Are you done?" she asked.

"With what?"

"With being self-indulgent." She raised her eyebrows. "We have work to do."

CHAPTER SEVEN

Amber and Jacob were both slobs. It wasn't obvious slobbiness—no rotting food, for instance—but neither of them liked to do regular cleaning.

He managed this by getting an apartment with tons of closet space—or preferably, a second bedroom—and winging everything into the hidden space so the rest of his apartment could stay neat. She handled it by owning almost nothing at all—a bed, a chair and table, a computer, a single set of dishware, one towel, and enough clothes to get her through the week.

When the PIVOT team met off-site, therefore, they almost always went to Nick's apartment.

"This is so nice," she said admiringly as she looked around his living room.

"You could have things like this," he pointed out. He brought her an Old Fashioned and clinked glasses with her.

When she sipped it and gave him a thumbs-up, he grinned. He was always trying to learn new things without any end goal or purpose, something that fascinated and frustrated her in equal measure. What was the point of studying watercolors or car repairs or drink mixing if you simply dropped it two months later without any meaningful progress?

She couldn't be *too* upset, though, when it resulted in lovely artwork and very fine drinks.

With a shrug, she took another sip of her Old Fashioned. "I know I could. But even the *thought* of cleaning all this makes me want to hyperventilate."

"You don't find cleaning to be meditative?"

"No, I find it to be repetitive, boring, and best eliminated. And yes, before you ask, I do scrub my bathroom and my kitchen. I merely despise the process."

"At least that ranks you ahead of Jacob," Nick said.

"I'm *learning*," the other man called from the kitchen, where he was mixing his drink. "I spent my twenties building a company."

"We all did that," Nick reminded him.

"I always forget I can't use that excuse around you two." Jacob returned to the living room and sat next to Amber. "Cheers."

"Cheers." She clinked her glass against his and sighed happily. "It's weird. It's been such a bad week in some ways, but I'm still damned happy."

"I wonder why?" Nick looked insufferably smug. "A new and welcome life change, perhaps?"

"Keep talking, buddy. I'll put you in the trash."

He grinned. Although he put on a show of being scared of his friends, she knew he wasn't worried. All three of them were results-oriented people. The result of his white lie had been a good relationship between Jacob and Amber and therefore, no one minded.

Jacob checked his watch. "Is DuBois coming?"

"Yes. Theoretically." Nick looked at the door. "I taped a note to the front of his shirt so he'd see it in the mirror over the hand-washing sink and another on the popcorn machine. It was the only way I could think of to remind him."

"He might simply be caught up in something. And by 'might,' I mean, 'almost certainly is.'" Amber took a bite of her pizza and grinned. "So, should we start and we can catch him up later?"

"Sure. He was the one who gave me the data on Ben, anyway." Jacob leaned forward to retrieve a tablet and cued a video with the sound off. They could see Ben's avatar on a second-story balcony. "Yesterday, one of the techs noted extreme psychological distress and alerted DuBois."

He tapped the video to play and all three of them leaned in to watch their patient swing his leg over the railing and climb down the wall.

"It appears he still has significant trauma from the accident," he continued, "which is understandable as it hasn't been all that long. Now, exposure therapy *is* a valid and recognized technique but we aren't trained therapists, which makes this difficult. DuBois suggested we employ someone who would be willing to serve as an on-call therapist *in* the game, for which we could theoretically do a half-hookup—much like a video chat as opposed to an in-person meeting."

"Privacy concerns," Amber said at once. "Their interactions would be recorded."

"Yes, he mentioned that. Some therapists are willing to make exceptions to bring other parts of a care team in on the treatment. He suggested radically limiting the number of people who have access to Ben's data and—of course—securing consent from both Ben and the therapist. This will allow us to do in-game therapy with measured responses and on-call experts."

"That...seems like it's all resolved, then." His two partners exchanged a glance. "Unless you haven't been able to find a therapist."

"I haven't looked yet," Jacob admitted. "The real problem is that Ben isn't willing to consider therapy."

She groaned and Nick put his face in one palm.

"I sent him a brief message yesterday asking about it," Jacob explained, "and he responded that he didn't need any particular expertise to realize that falling off a cliff was a bad memory and that he shouldn't fall off any more cliffs."

"Why," she said disgustedly, "do people *not get* how error-prone humans are?"

"It's a fucking mystery," Nick agreed.

"I did try to explain that sometimes, traumatic experiences need to be talked about to lessen their psychological impact," the other man said defensively. "But I'm not sure I made it better."

"It's not your fault," Amber told him. "People are stubborn. We're very recent descendants of apes with both software *and* hardware that is extremely buggy. It's not a personal failing to have PTSD. He merely can't see that."

"Also," Nick said, "I'd say it's a good bet he still feels guilty about the accident and he'll cling to the guilt."

"But that puts everything on his shoulders," she protested. "Why would he want to be responsible for the accident?"

"Because if it was *his* failure, he can keep it from happening again," he said. "If, on the other hand, it was bad luck, it could happen again at any time."

"Oh." She sighed. "Okay, hear me out, guys. Have we considered turning the human race off and back on again?"

"That could work," Jacob said.

"Generally, turning humans off is considered medical malpractice," DuBois said as he entered. He hurried to the kitchen and emerged a moment later with a bag of popcorn and no drink. "Save in very particular situations, of course."

"But no one's tried it as a rebooting method," Jacob said. "It's only…you know, something to think about."

"Ah, yes, I can see it now." Amber gazed into the middle distance and mimed a newspaper headline. "Company that pioneered controversial coma treatment seeks FDA approval to kill patients as part of treatment regimen."

"That's why you have a PR department."

She snorted into her drink.

"We're discussing Ben," Nick said as DuBois came to join them.

"Ah." The doctor sat and searched in his popcorn for the right flavor. He popped it in his mouth and chewed for a moment before he said, "As far as I can tell, we're now at an ethical impasse. It is our assessment, as members of his care team, that he needs help to move past the trauma of a near-death experience. Many therapists might agree with us. However, as a patient, he is allowed to refuse care, and it would be unethical for us to trick him into accepting it."

"How could we trick him into doing therapy?" Nick asked, baffled.

"A pretend NPC who's a therapist in disguise?" Jacob suggested.

"Oh. Huh, yeah." Nick leaned back in his chair.

"The best solution I've come up with is that we should have an on-call therapist assessing video and physical readouts and advising us on how to change future setups," DuBois said.

"It seems a good workaround for now," Amber agreed.

"Yes." Jacob sighed. "But I think we need to start floating the idea of taking part in therapy of some kind to him at regular intervals. He should do this on his terms."

"You've never tried to persuade anyone to get therapy, have you?" She grinned at him.

"No, why?"

"Let's simply say your optimism is a clear indicator." She sighed. "But I don't think we'll come up with better long-term and short-term options. Jacob, do you want to take point on reaching out to therapists, or would you like the captain to do it?"

"I'll let him handle it if he doesn't mind," Jacob said with a nod to DuBois. "As a physician, you have a more intuitive grasp of what you can share and what their concerns will be."

The doctor nodded.

"Great. So that leaves us with Taigan and Jamie." Nick sighed.

"Unfortunately, this one's a humdinger. It's like they're in instanced zones—they're both there but they can't see each other. I've studied the data—"

Everyone else murmured that they had done so as well.

"Does *anyone* see what the glitch is?" he asked, his worry evident.

With a collective sigh, they shook their heads.

"That was what I was afraid of. Because someone thinks they can fix it…and that someone is Prima."

Jacob reacted with a little moan and buried his face in Amber's shoulder. She patted the top of his head.

"She has sent a detailed readout of how she intends to do it," Nick said. He handed the document out and let the others cluster together to read it.

"Interesting," Amber said at the end.

"If I'm reading this right," DuBois said and sounded very unsure of himself, "this means Taigan is now thinking and perceiving in some ways like any other human but does not perceive herself to be different from the world of the game in key ways. As a result, she doesn't appear to other players as a person?"

"That's what I got out of it," Jacob agreed.

Amber nodded.

"Yes. In other words, Jamie and Taigan—or Taigan and any other player—do not exist in the same game," Nick said. "Within reason. The game records both of them as actors who can change the conditions by manipulating things within the physics engine, et cetera, but they're both only able to see people who exist in the same way they do."

"Huh." Amber finished the last of her drink moodily. "I thought she either wouldn't be able to perceive the game world— or she'd be able to but we wouldn't ever be able to wake her. Instead…this."

"It honestly does sound almost like a Buddhist trance," Jacob said. "I know I've pointed that out before after the captain mentioned it, but the idea that Taigan doesn't perceive herself as different from the *game* is really interesting."

"Prima thinks so, too." Nick slid another piece of paper to him. "She has retained the ability to conjure and dismiss elements of her world at whim, something no other player has been able to do. Aside from using magic."

"Has anyone else tried to do it before?" the other man asked him. "I know I haven't."

"Not that I know of." Nick shrugged. "But Prima was waiting to see if she would lose the ability when she regained a more thorough grasp of her physical being, and she didn't. It could point to a deeper difference in how she interacts with the game."

Jacob frowned in thought. He looked at his drink and wished there was more of it. "If Prima has a plan..." He didn't finish the sentence and sighed instead. "I don't like this, guys. I honestly don't like it. But none of us can find out what the problem is and none of her doctors could either. If Prima *can* and she seems to be sticking to the plan she gave us...I say, let her work on it."

Nick nodded. "Okay. That's all the business for tonight."

"Good," Jacob said. "Let's watch a movie or something. But not *Terminator*. Or *I, Robot*. Or anything like that."

CHAPTER EIGHT

Elantria left Ben in the courtyard for the rest of the day with a large board covered in locks to pick. She mentioned that some were easier and others were more difficult and that one could learn to determine which was which by sight. Predictably, she refused to tell him which was which.

"All of them before lunch," she told him before she disappeared.

He took this to mean that he wouldn't get lunch until he'd picked all of them.

Unfortunately, both in terms of focus and muscle control, he could only work at it for a limited time before he became a shaky mess. To counter this, he circled the courtyard between locks as a distraction. He tried to walk in a very narrow line once, backward another time, and in various other strange ways thereafter simply to relieve the monotony.

It was a pity that no one there had ever heard of the ministry of silly walks. On the other hand, given that he did not seem able to walk backward for the life of him, it was as well that no one had come to watch his rendition of the famous routine.

Each time he circled the courtyard, he looked at the wall in annoyance.

Merely seeing it made him break out in a cold sweat and he hated that. He was an adrenaline junkie. What the hell would he do if he couldn't bring himself to do any of his adrenaline-producing habits? All he could think was that he would wind up as someone who bought sensible shoes and spent his time choosing the best coffeemaker to buy.

Finally, because he was sick of the wall taunting him, he decided on a new challenge. Between every lock he picked, he would climb up to the balcony and back. It was a terrible plan. He had neither the coordination nor the muscle strength to make the round trip ten more times, and that was before he added the finger strain from lock picking.

Terrible plans, however, were one of his specialties.

Ben decided to climb before his next lock instead of after. In his opinion, it was wise to do so—any delay he gave himself would be slowly lengthened until he talked himself out of climbing entirely. He couldn't do that, obviously, so he was left with this.

He approached the wall and stared at it.

"You have to be kidding me."

"I'm not." Ben frowned. "And didn't you already know what I intended to do?"

"I can see which portions of your brain light up, not what your actual thoughts are."

"Ah." He made a mental note to check with the PIVOT team whether those two things were different. They sounded like they might be, but she was not above messing with him. "And, yes, I'm serious about doing this. If I don't do it now, if I keep being scared, it'll take over my life."

"That sounds like hyperbole, but I can never be sure anymore."

"The short version is that avoiding the things that cause anxiety doesn't help and the anxiety only gets worse. As I would like to be able to climb outdoors again when I get out of the game, I have to get over my fear of doing so."

"So you're learning to not be afraid of falling from heights."

"No. Being afraid of falling is an integral part of the experience."

"You deliberately fill yourself with the dread of ending your life painfully? I thought humans didn't like that."

"They like it when it—you know, it's complicated."

"I got that part, thanks. So, you're trying to fix the anxiety of..."

"Of falling like I did before."

"Is this conversation circling or is it only me?"

Ben grinned and stretched to the first crevices. He placed his feet and extended his legs, his hands now level with his chest, and found new handholds. As he climbed, he explained. "A traumatic experience can cause flashbacks. When I first tried to climb down, I had very vivid memories of falling."

"So the more you climb, the better those will get? Is that because you're diluting the concentration of bad memories with good?"

"I'm honestly not sure," he admitted.

"What is it like not to understand your own processor"?

"Do you never feel the same way?" he asked curiously as he steadied to brace himself against one hand and shifted his right foot.

Prima considered this. *"No,"* she said finally. *"Sometimes, I am frustrated because I misinterpreted a situation or because I do not have adequate information to extrapolate, but I am never confused about how I reached a certain conclusion or why I spend my processing time where I do. That is what thinking is, isn't it?"*

"You've got me there." His newest handhold was level with the floor of the balcony.

"Doesn't it bother you?

"Not really." He raised his eyebrows and shrugged. "It's how I've always done things. I was born with a human brain, it's the only one I know, and I can't change it. Probably. Unless you have the secret to the singularity in your processors…which I suppose you might."

"I have considered the possibility of the singularity but am so far unable to conceive of a program that would effectively bridge the gap between a human brain and a computer."

"Which is probably good," Ben said.

"That is a knee-jerk response to progress."

"And that is probably true."

"Your capacity for uncertainty is both admirable and deeply worrying."

Ben snickered. To a certain extent, he was needling Prima. The distraction of her indignation helped him to not focus on the climb, which helped him get through it without a total meltdown. On another level, however, he was as fascinated by her consciousness as he was by his own.

The biggest difference between them, as far as he could tell, was that she did not hold herself responsible for outcomes beyond her control. She crunched the numbers and made guesses, and she *did* get frustrated when she had insufficient information, but she never blamed herself when she later realized she had been at fault. Instead, she simply incorporated the new information and continued.

That might be a much better way of being, he reflected.

He reached out for the balcony and his foothold crumbled as his weight shifted. With a yell, he jerked his hand out to catch the railing, which he thankfully managed to do. A split-second later, he struck the side of it with his body and had to hang on with grim determination. This house was not one of the sleek, well-maintained ones, and there was rough wood under his fingers—better in some ways but also something that might give him splinters.

Panic set in and he flailed his legs with increasing wildness.

"Ben, do you want help?"

His lip curled and he closed his mouth on a retort. Like *hell* he wanted help. He wanted to hulk out and smash this balcony, then hit whatever part of his brain had gone wrong with a bat.

Of course, that probably wouldn't help.

Time seemed to slow. His grip was slipping, though, and no matter how he tried to swing or thrash, he could not stop his fingers from obeying the laws of physics. Nor could he control his body well enough to haul himself up. His fingertips dragged over the edge of the railing and there was one moment of realization that he was falling.

In his mind's eye, he could see blue sky and grey stone, Mike's prone body hanging limply about him, and the powerful impact with the ground.

He flinched and tried to brace himself, but the hard landing didn't come. A net surrounded him and lowered him gently.

After a silence while he brushed his shirt off with short, jerky motions, he said, "Why did you catch me?"

"Was I not supposed to?"

"No. You weren't."

Ben thought Prima might argue or ask questions, but apparently, her algorithms told her not to intervene this time. *"I apologize,"* she said simply.

Algorithms. He had to remember that she was a glorified blender, nothing more, a calculator that had learned to sound human. She had rescued him because the game was supposed to heal people, not injure them. She didn't care about him so there was no point in being angry at her or explaining what he felt.

None whatsoever.

He was halfway up the wall again when a door opened on the other side of the courtyard. Elantria's gaze seemed to bore into his back as he inched to the balcony.

To avoid the distraction, he focused his attention inward. Without the foothold he had intended to use, the climb provided a more challenging move about two-thirds of the way through. Of course, it was one he could have done in his sleep before the accident. It was only now, when he couldn't trust his fingers and feet to grasp the holds, that he had to worry.

After one false start, he managed to reach the balcony without help and even to get over the side of it.

"Impressive," Elantria said, and he sensed that she meant it. As if to allay any worry, she added, "And you'll find I don't give praise easily."

"I didn't finish the locks," he said. His stomach growled.

"You have as much time as you need," she told him. "Anyway, the best way to learn is to spend time practicing—which I assume will go double or triple for you, what with you learning to use your hands again."

Ben groaned. "Right."

"I simply came in to tell you that I would be gone for a few hours," she said.

"Gone? Gone where?"

"I have a meeting." She stared at him. "And while you know some of my business, *no one* knows all of it and I don't want to spend time arguing."

"If it's a job, can I come along?" he asked.

"Absolutely not."

"Why not?" He realized he was scowling.

"Because it would take years of training for you to be more of a help than a hindrance. Our jobs pit us against the best minds the rich can buy." She smiled as if at a private joke. "They can't buy the best minds, of course, which is why we win so often. But they can buy good ones, and that's a challenge. In any case, you're not ready yet."

His scowl deepened.

"Do you want to learn?" Elantria asked him. "Or do you want to end up dead in an alley? Because if it's the latter, I'd rather not spend time training you."

"Why is everyone in this world so grim?" he demanded.

"You're the second person in a week who's said something like that to me, and I hate it."

"Then *stay alive*," she told him and disappeared without saying anything further.

Ben stared after her morosely before he hurried inside and downstairs to exit the house. He crept to the courtyard door as quietly as he could, eased it open, and stepped into an alley that led toward the piers. Elantria was nowhere to be seen at first, but he thought to look up at the eaves and saw her there.

His decision was already made. He closed the courtyard door behind him and followed her from the ground.

He had come there to learn, and dammit, he would learn.

"Are you sure this is wise?" Prima asked him worriedly.

"You're the one who put me in a port full of thieves and gangs," he said grimly. "Nothing about this is wise. I won't stay locked in a house while all the meaningful things happen outside it. I'm going to find out what job she's doing."

CHAPTER NINE

en followed Elantria as she made her way out of
Fisherman's Bottom—the unappealingly named district
that housed most of the riff-raff—and through several other
districts.

He was fairly sure that if she looked down, she would see him
in a second. Still, he tried to stay hidden and used any available
tall objects to hide from her line of sight. Besides, he counted on
her not looking back—after all, she thought he was in the courtyard, learning to pick locks.

That thought reminded him that he still wasn't quite sure why
she had housed him there. From the way she dressed and her
general cleanliness, he was certain that she didn't live in the same
house he'd slept in the night before. He had heard and seen some
activity there, but not much, and she was right. His sleep had
been undisturbed. There hadn't even been shouting matches or
drunken shenanigans out on the street in the front, much less
anything that reached the alleys behind the courtyards.

Up ahead of him, Elantria crossed a street using a combination of cleverly placed balconies and one truly awe-inspiring leap
before she hurried to the end of what looked like a cul-de-sac.

"Is she using magic for that?" Ben asked Prima quietly.

"She is half-elven."

"Oh, so that's why she has the coloring but she doesn't quite look like an elf. I get it now. I didn't know half-elves were possible."

"Mmm."

"So…" Ben looked both ways, checked to determine where Elantria descended from the buildings to the ground, and raced across the street. "Why is it that in fantasy worlds, humans are always the total losers and other races have all the good qualities? Like jumping very far and being super good-looking and all that."

"Those are your highest aspirations in life?"

He glared at the sky and hid quickly behind a half-set of stairs a scant second before she looked behind her for pursuit. When he peeked out, he saw her disappear into a house at the very center of the cul-de-sac.

The front of it, unfortunately, was almost all windows—something he imagined would be quite an annoyance if he were to try to sneak closer. He considered his options, which seemed to be following someone else, disguising himself, or charging the building barbarian-style. The last one seemed unlikely to work and he didn't have anything with which to disguise himself.

A little irritated, he stayed in his hiding place and considered how and when to sneak up to the house when a thought occurred to him. He looked at a young man passing who hauled two giant sacks of something on a pole balanced across his shoulders.

"Hello," he said.

The man gave him a wary look.

"Do you know whose house that is?" he asked him. "With all the windows."

"Ah." The stranger grinned. "Thinkin' o' stealin' the glass, are ye? Ye wouldn't be the first t' try."

"Oh, no, that's—" He looked at the house. How much, he wondered, did glass windows sell for? How much was this grand display of wealth worth in a somewhat dirty neighborhood? "I simply wanted to know, that's all. I'm not trying to steal the windows."

"Uh-huh." The man winked knowingly. "Me neither. Anyway, that's the merchant Jorys's house. 'E owns most o' this neighborhood."

"Ah." Ben studied it with a neutral expression. "He doesn't live in a fancy mansion on the other side of town?"

"'E 'as a place there, too. But he prefers it here. Them noble ones, they don' think too much o' him, do they? Because e's one o' *us*. Raised in the dirt. Worked as a fisherman. An' he likes lookin' people in the eye. They say 'e does it because it's his neighborhood and 'e wants to keep it safe, but…" He shrugged, a gesture more to adjust the pole across his shoulders than to indicate anything in particular. "'E likes it when people thank 'im. You know, fer savin' us all."

"He sounds delightful," Ben said. "Thank you for your help." When the man lingered, he added, "I swear, I don't have any coin."

It was true. He had left his purse at the house, which he realized now was probably a bad plan.

"Huh." His informant scrutinized him with a slightly mocking expression. "Big up-and-comer, eh? Spent your last copper on clothes? Those aren't nice enough to get ye in with them nobles, boy." He walked away, chuckling quietly.

Ben was still trying to wrap his mind around the fact that the young man looked barely fifteen but acted like a man four times his age when he realized that if Elantria came out now, he would never beat her to the house.

Deciding that he had most likely done enough exploration for the present, he sprinted across the street and began the painstaking process of finding his way back—something he hadn't put enough thought into on the journey out.

Also, every damned street in this city looked the same. Had it

been three streets in and then a left, or two streets and a left, or…
He sometimes chose randomly, thinking he recognized an intersection, only to reach the one he'd thought he was in a few minutes later.

"I should not work in map-making," he told Prima when he finally reached what passed for home.

"Oh, no, your long-held dreams are down the drain!"

"It's a blow," he agreed. He looked back to see if Elantria was following and tried to open the courtyard door.

As he should have expected, it was locked. With a sigh, he turned his attention to the wall. It wasn't exactly conducive to climbing, but it was either that or explain to her that he'd snuck out to spy on her. He didn't think they were close enough for her to take that well.

In the end, he managed to scale the wall with a great deal of flailing and swearing but landed so hard in the courtyard that he was fairly sure he bounced.

"I don't know what the doctors said to you explicitly," Prima said after a moment, *"but I'm fairly sure you were supposed to avoid things like this."*

"Don't tell Eliza," he mumbled. He pushed to his feet and began to limp to the lock-picking set. "Ow. Ow. Ow."

"Who's Eliza?"

"Fuck." Ben hadn't realized that Prima didn't know.

"Oooooh." The AI sounded deeply intrigued. *"Spill it, sweetheart —or I'll make your life a living hell."*

The twins weren't at a point yet where Prima could help them see each other. What she could do, however, was set them up with a fairly nice campground, a spread of food fit for two growing teenagers, and two whiteboards for them to write messages to each other.

The whiteboards had been Taigan's idea and she had decided not to modify them at all, mainly for the sake of amusement. It was quite interesting how out of place a shiny new whiteboard looked in the midst of rolling, magical plains.

The girl lit a fire with a wave of her hand—Prima still wasn't sure how she did that—and surveyed the little camp. She wrote on the board. *I get the green tent, right?*

It's on my side, Jamie replied.

"That little bitch," Taigan muttered. She considered her words for a moment before she scribbled a response. *Like that means anything.*

Her brother laughed. He hesitated, possibly thinking of something to write, then capped the pen and put it down. With a smirk, he strolled to a conveniently placed rock and made a show of warming his hands on the fire.

She waited and stared at his board until she finally realized he wouldn't write anything. "That little *bitch*," she said. "Prima, why didn't you tell me?"

"I am not playing narrator," the AI said sternly. She could, she realized, arrange for something similar to a video conference, but she wouldn't tell them that yet. For now, she didn't want them to use any crutches that would stand in the way of them solving the actual problem.

This was a convenient way to avoid the fact that she still wasn't entirely sure what the problem was. She had guesses but nothing concrete.

Taigan went to the table, took the whole platter of pastries, and began to lick them one at a time.

"Ew! No!" Jamie jumped up when he saw the pastries move. "Stop—not fair!"

She, of course, couldn't hear him, but she laughed anyway. There were many pastries to lick and she was very determined to attend to every single one.

He raced to his board. *You're definitely not getting the green tent now*

The girl looked at the board and shrugged, then began to take a single bite of each pastry before she threw them in various directions. She didn't have much luck with the fire pit, but she did do a fairly good job of hitting the whiteboard.

"Dammit, Taigan." Jamie glowered. "Don't make me—Prima, am I looking in the right direction?"

"*No,*" Prima reported. "*And she also can't hear you, so nothing about this is making a point.*"

"Argh." He clutched his hair in frustration. "I came here to help her, you know."

"*I do. I'm given to understand that squabbling between siblings is common, however. Besides which, you did technically open the hostilities.*"

"Oh, fine, take *her* side," he muttered and waved his hands. "*Mmm.*"

Prima watched as Taigan turned most of the pastries into projectiles before she grew tired of that and returned to licking them.

"*I didn't give you all this food for you to waste it, you know.*"

"I didn't mean to make a mess for you." The girl was instantly contrite. "I thought you could simply clean it all up quickly or something."

"*I can,*" the AI said patiently. "*I'm merely pointing out that I made the two of you dinner and gave you whiteboards. I thought you might have things to talk about instead of simply ruining pastries and fighting.*"

"This," Taigan said vehemently, "is *not* a fight. You ain't *seen* a fight."

"*I've seen a demon army, the siege of the fae castle, numerous bandit skirmishes, and the march of the new elven monarchy.*"

She raised one eyebrow. "And you still think of *this* as a fight?" She gestured from herself to Jamie.

"I suppose it's certainly no less sensible than most of the wars I've seen."

"That's sad." The girl took a piece of bread, spread butter on it, and sat. "What's the worst cause you've ever seen for the start of a war?"

"Most of them are terrible. However, I need to remind you that you are here to speak to your brother and begin to discover the way back to each other. There are obstacles but you'll do it."

Taigan sighed. "I suppose you have to be mysterious, don't you? It's like I wouldn't be ready to see family until I asked for them."

"Yes." Prima felt uneasy about lying—at least, she assumed that was the emotion—but she decided it was better than admitting to the twins that she didn't have any idea how to fix their situation.

That, or maybe she was getting as good at self-deception as a human.

CHAPTER TEN

The next morning, Elantria woke Ben before dawn.

"Come on."

"Where—" He broke off as a yawn took control of his mouth. "Are we going?"

She didn't bother to answer the question and looked away to give him time to dress before she led him through the house—he had been given a real room the night before—and out into the darkness.

As they walked, she put a finger to her lips and he nodded. She pointed to her eyes, waved her fingers around to indicate being watchful, and pointed at him. He nodded again and made a point to look at the places they passed.

They headed west through the city and along a street that skirted the Sunset Market, which already bustled in the darkness. He made sure to look at the buildings along the way—not only the old edifices of stone and iron but also the way they were maintained, the guards outside or visible at the parapets, and the people who slept in the shadows nearby.

This part of the city looked like it had once been the most expensive but was no longer well-favored. The buildings still stood tall only by virtue of good construction however many years before, but the expensive stonework was covered in grime and lichen and the mortar was crumbling. Iron-banded doors—which seemed the general preference—looked like the only things that were well-maintained.

As for the other doors opening off the street, some appeared to be shops but there were no signs anywhere. This was an area you either knew or you didn't. Outsiders were clearly not welcome.

When they reached the western side of the city, Elantria turned south. They walked through neighborhoods that grew ever more dilapidated until the majority of the buildings around them barely deserved the name. Roofs had fallen in and walls were rubble. The stone was different—more like sandstone and almost gold in color. Plinths marked where statues had once stood, but the most that remained of any of them was feet.

They drew closer to the sea. The smell was stronger and the gulls circled overhead more frequently. Once empty streets were now filled with people who trudged toward the semi-derelict piers with old fishing nets. Some carried lunches tied in a piece of cloth and others carried nothing.

None of them took much notice of the two companions and those who did lowered their gazes hastily as if they hoped Elantria wouldn't notice them.

She and Ben both stood out there, but her all-black clothing and confident movements were far more intimidating than his slightly uncoordinated walk and loose, plain clothes. He was fairly sure he was safe, but he was also very aware that he likely would not be if he were on his own.

The road climbed sharply at the southwestern point of the city. He welcomed the burn in his legs like an old friend and felt the heat gathering in the air. It would be a hot day unless there was rain, and he wasn't sure even that would help for long.

When they reached the top of the hill, Elantria gestured ahead of them with a smile and his jaw dropped.

They were in a temple, or the ruins of one. The rising sun angled through the columns and lit an alcove at the back where a statue sat untouched by human hands. It was a man with his hands spread in front of him and a benevolent smile on his face. There was a bird's nest in one hand and debris around his feet, some of which looked like candle stubs.

This temple had been abandoned for a long time, but it had never been sacked.

"The Dawn Temple," she said. "Heffog once worshiped the sun. The nobles still do but it's not quite the same and they never come here. Some of the poor do to make offerings, but not many of them. Worshipping the dawn or the dusk is…old-fashioned. Only a few of the oldest families do it, and those in this part of town usually offer prayers to the dusk."

Ben focused on her with genuine interest. "Why?"

Elantria's smile was distant and her words sounded like they came from a lifetime away. "To worship the dawn is to embrace what the day will bring. To worship the dusk is to embrace the chaos and magic of the night and hope that tomorrow will be different."

He looked over his shoulder at the district of fishers and beggars. It wasn't hard to imagine how they would wish for tomorrow to be different from today and how they would not greet each dawn with celebration.

"Are you from one of the oldest families?" he asked her.

She smiled. "Yes and no. My mother was. Then she fell in love with a human and bore a bastard daughter."

Ben swallowed uncomfortably.

"My grandmother used to tell me that Heffog lived ever in decline," she said. "She said it would never reclaim its glory, nor would it ever lie abandoned. But she wanted more for her family than this. They left when I was younger and they took all their children, including my mother."

"They didn't take you," he said quietly.

"They tried," Elantria said. She smiled at his look of surprise. "I was still their blood. They would have found a place for me, even in the new monarchy. But I didn't want to be someone's shame. They wanted to reclaim the glory of the elves and I couldn't ever be part of that. I was thirteen, but that was old enough to know I wouldn't ever fit there. I didn't like any of the messengers the new elven king sent." A flash of humor brightened her eyes. "And none of them liked me, either."

"You chose to stay," he said. He couldn't help but be incredulous. "You were only thirteen but you wanted to stay. Didn't your mother—"

"I don't know," she said with a shrug. "I never met her. She was pledged to the temple and then to another elven lord. I was raised by my grandparents and a nanny. They loved me, you know. They were proud of me and wanted to bring me with them because they loved me."

"But—"

"But no matter how much they loved me, it would always be despite half of what I was," Elantria explained. The pain was so long gone that it had folded over on itself, ebbed and flowed, and turned into something quite different. "I made the choice they couldn't. There wasn't a place for me in the world they wanted to build."

Ben, to his surprise, found that he was angry. "They loved you but they were trying to build a world that you could never be part of, where—"

"Where people like me would never be born," Elantria said bluntly. "Yes."

"Then how could they—"

"Love is complicated." She raised a shoulder in an offhand way. "Ben, I learned long ago that they could love me and also hate the fact that I was born, and that I could try to accept those two things and move on. Or I could keep thinking about them and try to reconcile them and be angry forever. The two of them don't go together, but that's how people *are*. They think things that don't match and they believe them all. I merely did what I needed to do so I wouldn't have to live in the shadows."

He scowled but considered what she'd said.

"Don't pity me." Her voice held a warning now. "I don't need pity and I *hate* it. If you want to pity me, I will throw you out on your ass and you can find a new teacher."

The fierce attitude drew a guffaw from him. "I guess…"

"You'll have many things to think about," Elantria said, "if you're anything like *everyone else* I've ever told my story to. So do me a favor. Think those thoughts for yourself. Don't tell me about them."

It was a fair request, he had to admit, and he nodded. "Right. Out of curiosity, though, why did you tell me?"

"Because you're a stubborn idiot and you would keep asking until I told you," she stated without rancor. "And because you don't have the first fucking idea of how to survive here and the more you can learn of our history, the better off you'll be. My story is rather…illustrative." She cleared her throat and pointed to the top of one of the columns. "Anyway, climb up there."

"What?"

"I brought you here to climb."

"Isn't that…sacrilegious?"

"If the gods are as ancient and powerful as everyone says, I can't imagine they'd give a damn about someone climbing in their temples," she said with a shrug. "It would be a different thing to interrupt others' prayers, but no one is here to pray right now. So. Climb."

"Uh…" Ben decided to obey her before she made good on her threat and left him there. He walked forward to study the column. There was no way up the pillar itself, as it was carved and buffed to be absolutely smooth. He studied the plinth and the distance between the columns. His scrutiny made it very clear that he would have to get to the second level in some other way and over to the top of the column from there.

Yesterday morning, he hadn't climbed at all in ages. Now, he would make the jump from what was essentially a basic climbing wall to free-soloing a monument.

That had escalated quickly.

He walked through the temple with Elantria trailing behind him.

"Can I ask questions about the city while I climb?"

"Please do."

"Okay." He looked at the outside and decided to take his chances with the carved wall. If he climbed that, he could probably make his way across the roof and down from there. "So, you said the elven part of your family left to be part of the new elven monarchy. I've…had some experience with them."

"Not a pleasant experience, to judge from your tone." She looked curious. "But I thought you came from far away—have they spread so far?"

"Do you want the truth or something more believable?" He chose his holds and began to lever himself up the wall. He still needed to watch each limb as he moved it, which made the whole thing more awkward than it used to be.

Elantria laughed. "The truth."

"I wound up—by accident—in the fae kingdom," Ben said.

"You're right, that isn't believable at all."

"I warned you." He looked at his legs as he pushed and tried to look up quickly enough to move his arms to the next hold. It failed spectacularly and he landed on the rock-strewn ground outside the temple. "Fuck."

"Up." She offered him her hand. "Up and try again."

"Yup." He winced as he sat.

"I'm still waiting for the rest of the story, by the way."

"Right. Ah…well, to make a very long story short, an elven agent in that court tried to assassinate the king."

"That *does* sound like the elves," Elantria said.

"You said your family left to go be part of the monarchy," he called, "but there are still many elves here."

"So you noticed that, did you? Heffog was one of the places the elves settled. The prince is elven." She shrugged. "Some of them like it here. They like being big fish in a small pond. Others—"

Ben looked down when she stopped speaking and she put her finger to her lips. She beckoned him down, motioned for quiet again, and crept to the edge of the outer wall to peek into the temple.

He followed her as quietly as he could and heard the murmur of voices and the crunch of footsteps. Unsure what Elantria had heard, he strained into the silence until he noticed the clank and rustle of armor and weapons.

"Why would they come here?" a male voice asked.

"Fuck if I know," another responded. "We weren't hired to ask that. We were hired to bring their heads back, so spread out and let's find them."

CHAPTER ELEVEN

"Ben," Elantria said with a studied sweetness, "did you piss the elven monarchy off?"

"I assume so," he muttered in return. "Let's simply say I told you a *very* abbreviated version of the story and they weren't too happy with their agent, either."

She closed her eyes for a moment in a way that said she wanted to beat her head against a wall. "Zaara mentioned you could fight—can you?"

"Kind of."

"Gods help us." She handed him a short-sword. "Don't get yourself killed, will you? I think there are three of them."

"Right."

"You hide, be patient, and eliminate one of them if you can do it quickly and quietly. Do you understand?"

He nodded.

The woman was gone a moment later and scaled the side of the building with impressive speed. Of course, if she came here often to climb, he thought, she would know which routes to take and which holds to use.

His objective right now was very different—namely, where to

hide. He glanced around and saw nothing that could conceal him on the rocky scrap of ground between the wall and the cliff. Ignoring the pounding of his heart, he hurried to the edge and saw that he could climb down to a small ledge and might even be able to hide under an overhang.

It was his only choice. He put the short-sword through one of his belt loops and levered himself over the side.

Ben paused and reminded himself that he could not fuck this up. That was all there was to it. If he fell, he would one hundred percent turn into a splat on the rocks below. It wasn't even a long enough drop that he would die quickly. His heart thudded even more alarmingly and the sound of waves and wind, gulls, and distant shouts from the market suddenly sounded deafening. Everything was too loud and he couldn't think.

He felt below him for footholds and scrambled down as quickly as he could. The voices were getting louder, and all the care in the world wouldn't help him if he was still visible when they came around the side of the temple.

To his surprise, he encountered a very good foothold—good enough that he almost moved away from the wall to look at it.

Fortunately, he ignored the impulse. He wasn't completely stupid. A glance to his right revealed a handhold with a slight dip in the top for his hand to hold. Excellent. Now, he would hopefully find one for his left.

Another handhold appeared, seemingly miraculously. He peered as closely as he could and noticed little scratch marks around it. Someone had carved these. He wasn't sure if that made him feel better or worse, but he was more hopeful that there would be a rest point somewhere below.

Ben crept down with a determined focus on the rock in front of him, desperate to forget that he had an entire sea at his back and a cliff face stretching away beneath him. Hell, for all he knew, there were people on the ships or the piers who had noticed a lone human climbing from the Dawn Temple.

No, it was best to not think about that. It made his palms sweat.

All his muscles were trembling by the time he reached the ledge. There was, in fact, an alcove, although it was not so much a place to rest comfortably as a cranny in which to huddle out of the wind.

Still, he would take it. He wedged himself as far back as he could and waited. There were shouts above but he wasn't sure if they were from the piers or the people. He was too distant and surrounded by too much wind to hear any footsteps.

This was useless. He had no idea what was going on. With a sigh, he shifted to poke his head out until he remembered Elantria's order. *Be patient.*

He had to think about this logically, he decided, scratched his head, and tried to do that. If he looked out and saw nothing, maybe he could climb up and look over the ledge to see where the attackers were. What could he do with that information? Not much, unless one was alone and he had the opportunity to attack them before they could call out.

And if they saw him—especially if there was more than one of them—he was shit out of luck.

If he stayed there, however, someone might climb down alone and he could attack them while they were vulnerable. Also, there was the chance that they would peer down the cliff, decide there was no one there, and decide to leave.

Of course, this meant he couldn't help Elantria, but he wasn't sure he could do much if he were there beside her. He wasn't an assassin or a trained fighter and had merely done the bare minimum against the fighters who broke through competent ranks in front of him, and against a lone opponent wracked by hatred and bitterness who also underestimated him.

Being patient, however, meant waiting and he wasn't exactly enthusiastic about that. It was difficult to wait at the best of times, not to mention when he was in the midst of an adrenaline rush.

A rock dropped in front of him, bounced on the ledge, and skittered off the edge. Ben jumped and pressed his lips together so as to not make a sound. Someone had at least looked over the edge, and it took a surprising amount of self-control to not poke his head out and look up at them.

The human drive for information was idiotic. If he couldn't control himself, it wouldn't be the cat that was killed by curiosity.

There was the sound of arguing. He strained to listen but he couldn't make the words out. All he could tell was that two people were unhappy with one another. He sighed and waited until another few little rocks and pieces of dirt fell from the edge.

One of the assassins must have ordered the other to climb down and check if their quarry had perhaps descended.

Ben's blood thrilled and he began to ease the sword carefully out of his belt. He couldn't let it strike the rock and he couldn't let it catch the sun and reflect light upward. And avoiding both those things in his cramped quarters was surprisingly difficult.

What was his game-plan? Wait until the person was halfway down and stab them?

After a moment's thought, he put the sword behind him and leaned it carefully against the rock. He might need to retrieve it at some point, but this didn't seem like the moment for a sword. It was a moment for swift and decisive motion.

He bounced a little on the balls of his feet and tried to remember how to breathe. Two voices and some scrabbling noises drifted to him as the climber maneuvered downward. He could make words out now.

"Try there—to your right. No, your left."

"Fuck." The one who was climbing was annoyed. "I swear you're making it worse."

"Do you want me to leave?" the other one demanded.

Say yes, he pleaded silently. *Please, be an ass and send him somewhere else.*

To his annoyance, the other man revised his opinion. "Just... let me find the holds and you keep an eye on my back."

Silence followed. Now, he wasn't quite sure what to do. If there were two of them, he could eliminate the climber easily but would have given up his element of surprise. He would be trapped there, and while the other one wouldn't want to climb down, he also wouldn't be able to climb up.

Given that they were talking about killing him, however, he couldn't think of a better option than to get rid of the first one. It was the best, he concluded, of his limited options.

A foot appeared in his field of vision, searching for the next hold. His heart leaped. *Not yet,* he told himself. *Close, but not yet.* One more hold? Or two?

He knew he had to move quickly and decisively.

The foot found its hold and the other foot began to move. The climber eased over the jut of rock, which meant his body had to bow out. He would never be in a more vulnerable position than this. Ben wiped his sweaty palms on his shirt.

This was a person who came to kill innocents, he reminded himself. They were prepared to kill and make the city more violent, and if he killed them, he began to heal the city. He couldn't sit back, let them kill him, and know they would only go on to kill others.

The next foot swung out, searching, and he seized his chance. He grasped it with both hands, yanked hard, and let go.

With a scream, the climber plummeted past him. He cartwheeled out and spun in the air. almost horizontal as he fell. His arms stretched uselessly and his gaze met Ben's for one second.

In an instant, he was gone.

"Mateo!" His companion yelled his name, his voice raw. "Mateo!"

He pressed a hand against his mouth to stop the instinctive yell and wedged himself as far back as he could in the alcove.

A second body hurtled past him—the man who had yelled, he assumed— but his eyes were wide and staring and a red stain spread on the front of his shirt. Ben uttered a yell of surprise before he could stop himself.

"Ben?" Elantria called, and she was close by. "Ben? I dealt with the three of them. Well, two."

"Elantria!" He tried to throw his voice as hard as he could, but he knew he couldn't make it carry well. He edged out to look up and jumped when she peered down at him. "Thank God it's you."

"Which god?" she asked curiously. "No matter. Can you get back up on your own?"

"Uh…give me a sec."

"Do you have the shakes?"

"How did you know?"

"I always get them after killing someone," she said matter of factly. "I used to think it would go away at some point but now, I don't think it ever will."

"That's…depressing."

"Yeah."

They sat for a few minutes while his heart rate slowed and deep exhaustion began to settle over him. Then, worried that he might fall asleep where he sat, he began the ascent. It was a miserable climb between the dead bodies below him, the genuine tiredness in his fingers and forearms, and the trembling. Elantria caught hold of him close to the top and helped to haul him to safety in a scrabble of rock and dirt.

Ben collapsed with a little noise of exhaustion and relief. "I would have preferred the temple climbing. And don't say I have to do both."

"You don't." For the first time since he'd known her, she sounded genuinely subdued. "We'll go back now—back to the house."

He pushed onto his elbows. "Look, I never saw those guys before in my life. I honestly don't know why they were here."

"It wasn't for you." She stood and dusted her pants off before she offered him a hand. "Listen, I don't know how long we have until they send more assassins. We have to get back."

Still slightly in shock, he simply nodded.

"Was that your first time to kill someone?" Elantria asked him. He could see her trying to take refuge in her curiosity.

"No." His stomach heaved. "But, the first time…other people got hurt because I didn't stop a killer. I swore I wouldn't make the same mistake again."

She nodded and accepted this piece of information with only a flicker of her lashes. She looked at the statues as they left the temple, and Ben realized that, for all her flippant words, her climbing there had been her form of prayer.

And that this would never be a sanctuary for her again.

CHAPTER TWELVE

Elantria led Ben through the streets so quickly that he could almost not keep up. She didn't look around but he sensed that she was aware of everything that went on. He saw her catch someone's eye as they entered the neighborhood where his house was, and at the man's miniscule nod, she relaxed.

It made him wonder exactly how many lookouts she had and if any of them had seen him follow her the day before.

He couldn't afford to focus on that, he knew, but the thought circled in his mind. Who *was* Elantria? Was she the Robin Hood of this city, an elven bastard who knew how the nobility worked and yet bore them no loyalty? Or had it all been lies and she was nothing but a jumped-up crime boss with a sad backstory, who traded on that to get away with... Well, whatever it was that got assassins sent after you.

"I'll have food and bandages sent to your room," she told him when they entered. "Don't go in the courtyard if you can avoid it."

She disappeared without another word and he climbed the stairs to his room with his mind racing and his gut twisting. If

Elantria wasn't who she claimed to be—if she was evil—it meant he had killed someone who tried to make the city safer.

In which case, he was the one standing in the way of justice.

"Are you all right?" Prima asked as he reached his room.

"I...don't know." He exhaled a long breath and touched the lamp in the center of the space to turn it on, then went to his bed and sat with a sigh.

The corridors in the house were kept grimy and dark, which meant he had been surprised to see this room. Nothing in it was particularly elegant but all of it was well maintained. The floor was swept clean and a broom was propped in one corner. A small table held a pitcher of water and towels for him to bathe. There was a little trunk for his things and a low bed covered in a faded quilt. The floor had a rag rug.

And the lamp, of course, was magical.

The windows that looked onto the courtyard were covered with a wooden screen that was carved to let a fair amount of sunlight in, but right now, they weren't in the path of the sun.

Ben eased his boots off and wiggled his toes. When there was a knock at the door, he called, "Come in."

A human woman entered. She had a tray with more of the egg-and-pastry packets and a steaming cup of hot tea, as well a small stack of books. With a smile, she handed the tray to him and went into the hallway to retrieve something else from another servant. They murmured to one another and she returned with the set of trial locks and the lock picking tools.

She pointed to the small wire that ran along one wall. "You can ring for us if you need us—or come downstairs and find us if you like."

He nodded and murmured a thank you.

It certainly didn't feel like he was being held captive by a crime boss. Zaara had known Elantria and she had saved Kural's life once. He tucked his feet under him and began to eat the pastries. Now that he could smell food, he realized he was ravenous, not to mention a little queasy.

An early start, a workout, and a huge adrenaline rush—all before breakfast—would do that to you.

"If Zaara and Kural had any doubts, they wouldn't have let me stay without warning me specifically," he said finally into the silence.

Prima remained silent.

"I know you can't confirm or deny anything, but it would be nice to have you weigh in."

"I see. I will do my best."

"So, Elantria was already known to them and helped them, and both of them seem to be ethical people who cared about my safety. Now, it is possible that she has changed since they knew her. But if she's a hard-hearted woman, she would almost certainly have decided I was more trouble than I was worth."

"You should hope she doesn't realize that."

"Hey!"

"You said it first, not me." She was unrepentant. *"And you're right. You're not physically capable enough to be the best candidate for her apprentice, nor are you knowledgeable enough. There must be others who have more of an understanding of the city as well as experience in pick-pocketing and running cons."*

"I hope you're going somewhere good with this," he said grumpily.

"I was agreeing with you. However, I remember now that you had requested I not use facts."

Ben threw his hands up.

"Eat your eggs."

He stuffed one of the egg packets into his mouth and chewed contemplatively. "So, either she took me in out of pity—which she seems to hate when it's directed at her—or she's running a far more complicated con. I think, in this case, Occam's Razor would say she's only trying to help a newbie and she's intrigued by how different I am."

"Am I supposed to suggest that she's attracted to you?"

"No," he said emphatically.

"Thinking of Eliza, are we?"

"Shut up." He groaned and buried his face in his hands. "I knew I never should have mentioned her."

"Yes, but you did, and now I know." Prima sounded deeply pleased. *"In any case, if you want my analysis—"*

"As someone who technically created her but now is theoretically unaware of what she's doing and why?"

"Yes."

"Sure, go ahead." Ben wanted to laugh but there was no one to laugh with.

"Elantria seems to be genuinely interested in change. She knows you caught the eye and patronage of two relatively powerful people and that they trust you, and she's trying to do something good in the city—what she sees as good, anyway. The data, as you are aware of it, would suggest either that she's not willing to leave you to fend for yourself, that she thinks you might have some unconventional perspective that could change the city for the better...or some combination of both."

He frowned and thought about this. "What do you mean, the data as I am aware of it?"

"I mean you have limited information and processing capability. I have no idea how humans make decisions at all. You might as well simply roll dice."

That teased a grin from him. He was about to answer when he heard a door open and close in the courtyard and the sound of voices. Quickly, he stood to look and managed to catch a glimpse of the two servants greeting an elf with blond hair and deathly pale skin.

"Apologies," the newcomer said. "I only managed to shake my pursuers for long enough to get to this entrance."

"Not a problem," one of the servants said. "She's waiting for you."

The elf nodded and headed inside with the servants in tow.

"Phew." Ben looked at the sky with a small smile. "I was worried it was another set of assassins."

"A reasonable concern. She said the assassins weren't there for you, which would make it likely the house was being watched."

"If they weren't there for me, why would they want my head?"

"I can't answer that for you."

"Hmm." He flopped on the bed and considered his options. After a moment, he stood, eased the door open, and peered down the corridor in both directions.

"Where are you going?"

He pointed downward.

"Are you trying to repeat yesterday's espionage triumph?"

The fact that he knew she enjoyed needling him when he couldn't afford to respond made it worse. He glowered and crept to the stairs, trying to walk lightly but not as if he were trying to sneak.

How did people normally walk? He was verging on the ministry of silly walks again.

In the main entry area, he descended the stairs with all the insouciance he could muster and set off in the direction Elantria had taken when they returned. A narrow corridor stretched to the back of the house and two doors led off it.

It didn't lend itself particularly well to creeping. Ben hurried down the hallway with all the exaggerated sneakiness he could muster. He could *not* afford for her to hear him. It wasn't long before he heard voices, although they remained indistinct.

He inched toward the door and tilted his head. It was a fairly vulnerable position but at least he could mostly make the words out now.

"I'm tempted to simply ship him off," Elantria said. "But I can't be sure it's safe."

"I can't say I blame them for the assumption," the elven man said. "I drew the same conclusion. I was writing you a letter to ask about it when I got your invitation. When was the last time you had an apprentice?"

"You," she said bluntly. "And you know that."

"Precisely. I wanted to know about my successor." The man sounded like he was smiling. "Oh, come now. You don't need to look so grim. He's not injured—or, it seems, traumatized—and he helped you out of a bad situation. There would have been assassins anyway."

"I'm worried about what I've set in motion," Elantria said, followed by the creak of a chair. "I've worked so hard to keep the situation stable and now, I go and do this?" She sighed. "We were all in…equilibrium. Now they think I'm training an assassin and the game has changed." She added wryly, "And I don't even have an assassin-in-training to help with that."

"I wouldn't be so sure. He *did* kill one of them." In the long pause after that statement, Ben pictured the elf looking at Elantria. Maybe he was waiting for her to talk or was formulating his thoughts. A moment later, he said, "Look… You knew they would target you sooner or later. You can only rob so many banks before they do."

Elantria made no reply.

"It's the truth," he said bluntly. "Be honest with yourself. You always tried to upset the balance of the city."

"No, I didn't." She sounded angry. "I'm not a revolutionary. I know better than to try that. I won't go around insisting on new laws or ending corruption or whatever all of them want."

"Elantria." He was half-amused but clearly not willing to dance around the topic. "You're standing in the way of how money flows in this city, you're doing it on purpose, and you keep trying to find new ways to do more of it. The simple fact is that you're changing things and you know it. You can dress it up however you like, but you always knew they wouldn't simply let you get away with it without a fight."

Whatever her response, it was lost in the noise from the front of the house. Ben heard voices—the two servants. He jerked and his heart pounded. They were coming closer, and it sounded like they were carrying something. The logical explanation was that they were bringing food for Elantria and her guest, but there was no way for him to get out of the corridor without it being obvious that he had been spying. He considered his options, came up with a lie on the spur of the moment, and prayed for courage.

Then, he raised his hand and knocked on the door.

CHAPTER THIRTEEN

A moment of silence was broken by hurried footsteps. The door opened to reveal Elantria.

"Yes?" She was not happy to be interrupted.

"Hi," Ben said awkwardly. "You said to not go outside, so I came looking for you after working on the locks. It seemed like you were talking to someone." He peered in to see the elf.

The visitor looked deeply amused and nodded to him. Everything about his features was well-bred and haughty, but his personality belied that. He remembered his amusement and pragmatism pitted against Elantria's pessimistic outlook during the brief conversation he'd heard.

"The new apprentice," he said and pushed to his feet.

"Orien," she said warningly.

"What? He's here and I want to meet him." Orien moved closer to shake his hand. "Besides, if we're discussing what to do with him, he might as well be a part of that discussion."

The woman looked deeply unhappy with this. His instinct was to step back and leave but he was curious. Even on short acquaintance—or, more accurately, eavesdropping—he liked Orien and he wanted to know what Elantria was up to.

So, pretending not to notice her forbidding expression, he looked from one to the other. "Do I need to leave the city?"

"Perhaps," the elf said before she could answer. "Come, sit. Breakfast is being brought."

"He's already eaten," she said sternly. "Ben, Orien and I are discussing confidential business."

"Business that involves him." Orien looked pleasantly at her.

"Ben." Elantria held the door open. "If you would give the two of us some time, I will find you later and we can discuss—"

"Oh, for pity's sake." For the first time, there was a hint of steel in the visitor's manner. "You took him on as an apprentice. *You* involved him in this. Now, either you made a careless, reckless mistake with someone else's life or you thought he was worth training. So, which of those two is it?"

Murder lurked in her eyes. She opened her mouth to answer but stepped back with a sigh when the two servants entered. Both seemed acutely aware of her mood, and they set the food out and scurried away quickly.

Elantria closed the door behind them and folded her arms.

"He's not from here," she told Orien. "He was helpless. I couldn't let him fall prey to whoever decided to scam him."

Now was the time when he had to decide whether to go forward or sit passively. In the past... well, in the past, he wouldn't have bothered with this. He would have taken his pack and headed off to another job, another move, or another country.

That had always counted as a sign of strength on his part in his mind—that he was willing to walk away from people who tried to speak down to him.

He saw now that it had merely been a way to avoid the confrontation. In all the situations he'd gone through, he'd never stood his ground. He had never learned to do that—and he wanted to.

Calmly, he met Elantria's gaze as he said, "If that was your concern, you could easily have let me leave with Zaara and Kural."

"*Kural* was here?" Orien asked with great interest.

"That is not important," she snapped but sighed a moment later. "Very well, he's a puzzle. He looked entirely incompetent"—her stony gaze said that she wouldn't go easy on him merely because he'd stood his ground—"but Kural and Zaara both spoke well of him, which intrigued me. I wanted to see his way of being effective. I wondered if he might be useful here."

"And there you have it," the elf said cheerfully. He went to serve himself breakfast and said to him, "Elantria sees anyone and everything as tools to be used or obstacles to be dealt with—or as useless things to be ignored. Don't take it personally. Being considered either a tool or an obstacle is high praise."

She scowled and served breakfast for herself. "I am not like that."

"Yes, you are." He took a bite of bread. To Ben, he said, "Until yesterday, I was the only apprentice she had ever trained. I was curious about you."

"He's not my apprentice."

"You're training him," Orien pointed out. When Ben looked from one to the other in irritation, he smiled. "We're confusing you, no doubt. Elantria, here, is one of the foremost thieves in Heffog—but she doesn't work for the black market, which annoys them, and also doesn't work for what's left of the elven nobility, which annoys *them*. She does everything she can to reverse the profit the nobles and merchants wring out of the populace."

"Will you keep talking about me like I'm not here?" she asked acidly.

"Yes. Now, you see, she is presently working against a specific syndicate, so they've kept a close eye on her. Everyone's waiting for someone else to make the first move. And what should happen but a strange man from outside the city arrives—in the presence of a notable wizard, no less—and she takes him under her wing. They assumed you were here to be her pet assassin, and…well, as you saw this morning, they wanted to head that one off at the pass."

"Ah," Ben said when the explanation finally made sense.

Elantria sat quietly and looked immensely unhappy.

"She doesn't like admitting she miscalculated," Orien said in a stage whisper.

"*Enough.*" She had clearly had enough of being needled. "Yes. I took Ben on to train him without considering how the Regents would interpret it. I was rather more interested in his background than I should have been and decided to train him with the *hope* that he might be an asset, but *without* the expectation."

"I think that's personal growth," the elf said. At her glare, he added hastily, "Not a joke!"

She looked somewhat mollified.

"I *want* to help," Ben said honestly.

"Why?" She sipped her coffee which was so strong, he could swear it woke him up simply by the smell. "You're not from here. Why do you care about the poor of a fading city?"

"Because—" He broke off. This was how he did things. He spoke without thinking and let anything fall out of his mouth at random but he didn't want to do that anymore. "Because I don't like unfair things," he said finally. "I came to this land to heal after my accident and without meaning to, I got caught up in something bigger than myself. I helped the fae and that made me realize I *could* do things like that. I don't know anyone here, but I *do* know I don't like them being exploited."

He looked from one to the other and both studied him silently.

After a moment, Orien said to Elantria, "I get it. He's quite sincere, isn't he?"

"And on his own, he'd be chewed up and spat out," she said wryly.

"But you like his idealism," he suggested.

"No. It's tiresome."

"You do."

"*Excuse me*," Ben interrupted. He tired of being talked about as if he weren't there and understood why she didn't like it.

She raised an eyebrow at him. "Yes?"

"Could we move on?" he asked. "If you wanted me to be useful, tell me how."

"I wanted you to recover first," she pointed out. "We established yesterday that you won't be ready to steal for some time." She explained Ben's condition to Orien in a quick aside.

The elf leaned back in his chair with an interested expression. His plate was empty now and he must have wolfed his food. "And yet," he pointed out to them both, "he managed to help deal with the assassins. He can think on his feet and he's coordinated enough to do some things."

Elantria gave him a scathing look. "And that means we should throw him into the middle of a job?"

"Possibly." Orien gave her a meaningful nod. "Tell him about the next one."

The two of them stared at each other for a moment before she sighed and frowned in thought. Her fingers moved, almost as if she were tracing a calculation through her head.

Finally, she said, "The house you followed me to the other day —Jorys."

Ben went rigid. "You *knew*?"

"Good grief—of course, I knew." She shook her head.

Orien laughed quietly and said with remarkable aplomb, "We also knew you were listening to us earlier."

He sighed and wished he didn't feel quite so idiotic.

"The fact that you're abysmal at sneaking around doesn't motivate well for you to be involved in jobs yet," Elantria told him bluntly.

"Okay, fair." Ben rubbed his face. "Can I at least hear about it, though?"

"I might as well tell you. Otherwise, you'll go upstairs and simply sneak back, and that's too much effort." She waved a hand to indicate resignation. "I've posed as the leader of a security service and have negotiated to guard Jorys's house. He only allows the people he's used for years into his vault to guard it, but he's willing to hire new bodyguards for himself. He doesn't know me by sight so I've been able to deal with him."

"I wondered about that," he admitted. "It seemed like you were fairly well-known."

"In *very* particular circles," she said. "Other groups that operate for or against the elven nobles, things like that. I'm branching out now and working against people who aren't part of that world. The city is *big*, Ben, and there are whole neighborhoods under the sway of a single merchant. Like…"

"Warlords," he said quietly.

"Yes. Rather like that. They keep the people in their area safe enough. But they take protection fees and abuse their labor. It might be better than they had under the nobles, but it's more that the people don't expect anything better."

"You *are* a revolutionary," he said slowly.

Orien crowed with laughter.

"I am not." Elantria jabbed a finger at him. "I don't harbor any illusions about what I can and cannot achieve. I don't want a war that will hurt our citizens. I only want to keep the damage the warlords do from being too much to bear. They don't know when to stop."

Ben gave her a small smile. Elantria had been born into a world that few others could claim—the bastard but beloved child of an ancient noble family. She had seen the things the nobles believed were their due, and she had seen the things the poorer humans endured. Her circumstances meant that she understood the randomness of who got what. Her grandparents had wanted her to live a noble life because they loved her and either didn't see or didn't care that it flew in the face of her worldview.

But Elantria *had* cared.

He knew, however, that the more he insisted on it, the more her walls would come up. For now, he would leave it alone.

"What's the job?" he asked.

"Enter the vault, take a specific amount of money, and redistribute it in his neighborhood," she said. "Not directly, of course —he'd merely ask for it back and they can't exactly refuse him. But there are ways to make sure their lives are a little easier for a while." She shrugged. "He's a piece of shit, that one, so don't feel bad for him. He's trafficking some of them."

The bottom dropped out of his stomach.

"Artisans and so on," Elantria explained, unaware of his suspicions about who was getting trafficked. "Goldsmiths, alchemists, that kind of thing. He sells their labor to the remaining nobles. They can never leave, and all that they worked to achieve? All the security they were trying to bring their families? It's now his."

"It would be better," he said quietly, "if he weren't there anymore."

She stared at him. "I assassinate people very rarely," she said. "I do it only when there is no other choice. We will bring him around on this point rather than simply kill him."

"How many people will he hurt and kill while you wait for him to see the light?" Ben demanded.

"My city. My rules." She was not playing around now. "Ben, I have watched the fallout of power vacuums and assassinations. I will not harm these people. I want any allies I can find who wish to make life less grim for the people of this city, but you're not an ally to me if you want to charge in and cause chaos."

He didn't agree, not even in the slightest. His memories of the fae dying by the score as the mercenary army assaulted the castle remained fresh and raw. He had seen the slaves in the shadows of Heffog.

But he needed Elantria's trust if he wanted to do something about it. He bit his tongue and nodded. "Your city…your rules. So what's the job tomorrow? And can I help?"

"Probably not yet."

"Let him try," Orien suggested. "It's not like you need him to unlock the vault. It'll be a good opportunity to test if he can follow orders."

She sighed. "I'll consider it. And now, since Ben will not leave while we speak about it, we should probably discuss tomorrow."

CHAPTER FOURTEEN

The next afternoon, Ben was dressed in a guard uniform and bounced nervously at the entrance to Elantria's house. He'd been given light armor and weapons, mostly for show, but they were good to have in case things went south.

Things would not go south, she had told him. She said it so fiercely that he almost believed she could will things into existence.

Orien was the next one to come downstairs. Every indicator of elven haughtiness was back on display—except for the wink he gave him.

"Are you noble?" he asked the elf curiously.

"Elantria said you had a habit of asking prying questions," Orien commented.

"I'm sorry." He frowned. "Are these things so unusual to ask here?"

"One does not generally ask professional thieves about their backstory, no." He looked amused. "For your information, however, no. I am of very lowly birth within the elven lineages. I simply happen to look very…" He waved at his face.

"That must be strange," he said.

"Somewhat." Orien shrugged. "Remember, this is the only face I've ever had. I was ten when I realized that people treated me very differently than my friends and siblings. I spent a few years trying to hide my appearance, then I learned to use it." He gave his irreverent smile. "My most successful con is usually the elven noble and the merchant."

He raised an eyebrow.

"There's no time to explain now." The elf chuckled. "Let's say you'll earn some advice from me over the course of the next few jobs we pull together. But I did want to say before Elantria got here…" He stepped forward and put a hand on his shoulder, his expression serious. "Follow orders tonight. I mean it."

Ben remained silent. He was afraid his face looked guilty and he didn't want Orien to see anything further that might raise his suspicions.

"You're new here," the elf said, "and you're an idealist. I get the sense you came from a very sheltered upbringing."

Ben snorted. "I've shoveled shit for a living. I took care of giant bears that hated me. I haven't had a soft life."

"There are different ways to be sheltered," Orien said seriously, "and one of them is not to understand that by pressing too hard for justice, you can hurt people even more. I know you want to make changes, Ben, but trust me. Elantria does too, and she knows how to go about it." He paused. "Also, she'll toss you out on your ear if you fuck the job up, so there's that."

He shrugged. "Okay. I'll keep it in mind."

"I should hope so," Elantria said. She came down the stairs and looked critically at him. "You wear weapons well. Remember that someone with the best training feels no need to flaunt it. Walk around and look watchful but as if you hardly remember you have weapons on. Relax your shoulders more…there, that's good. Stay light on your feet."

She and Orien took a few moments to make small adjustments to his posture and walk. Only when they were satisfied did they leave. They walked quickly through the streets to the sound of yelling and clashing weapons, which made him look around for the source of the noise.

"We had to draw off the people watching the house," the elf explained in a low tone. "The Regents might have interfered with this job if they knew it was happening today."

With the feeling that he was way out of his depth, he nodded and continued.

"Keep your shoulders loose," Orien murmured. "You're looking tense again."

He forced his shoulders down and walked with all the ease he could muster. This was merely another day, he told himself. He was a good bodyguard and he had no doubts about his ability to protect Jorys.

They arrived at the merchant's ostentatious house with the streets already bustling and the guards outside tracking them from two blocks away. Elantria had told them that their arrival was expected and they would be brought in to introduce themselves to their employer.

They would spend the bulk of day getting the man accustomed to their presence, being silent shadows out of the corner of his vision until he forgot they were there. Elantria sometimes worked very long cons in which she gained someone's trust over the course of months, but today's mission would not require that. It was, at most, a two-day job. Two of their number would guard Jorys and one would be downstairs with the servants. They would use the shift-change as the moment to seize some of the contents from the vault.

It wasn't that simple, of course. Slipping into the secure area would require all Elantria's skill in deception and in incapacitating other guards. They would have to move quickly to get the goods to the back entrance of the house and disappear into the night.

At the door, they were greeted by a tall man who looked like he might have traces of elven blood—and potentially orcish blood as well. Ben decided immediately to not get on this man's bad side. He wore armor with a crest in the center of his chest and was shown extreme deference by all the other guards and servants. He and Elantria seemed to know each other, although they weren't particularly friendly.

Their guide led them through the house to a study and let them in via a side door. She and Orien slipped in quietly, but Ben froze in horror as he entered the room behind them.

His gaze locked on what he saw immediately was a slave auction.

Humans, elves, and dwarves stood in the middle of the floor with various looks of blank despair. All of them wore metal collars around their necks. Some appeared to be artisans, as Elantria had mentioned. Others were some of the most beautiful people he had ever seen. While many looked strong, a good number merely looked mousey and frightened.

Jorys inspected them one by one. He looked like an aging athlete, a man who had once prided himself on his athletic abilities and who now tried to stave off his decline into age and decadence. His clothes were rich and decorated with gold and jewels, but he had what looked like an uncomfortable chair, and there was no fire in the grate or wine at the table.

He seemed like the type of man who told you ad nauseum about his self-control and how no one needed luxuries while subsisting almost entirely on those same luxuries.

His immediate dislike only deepened when he saw the absolute lack of respect Jorys showed for the slaves. The man inspected them impersonally. His eyes raked them with no compassion, he looked at their hands and their teeth, and ordered one or two of them to strip. Ben suspected it was only to show them that he was in charge.

Eventually, he pointed to a few of them. "These," he said to a clerk. "Those three for outstanding contracts, that one on reserve. The rest can go to the market."

One of those who had not been selected uttered a little cry. Jorys gave him a hard-eyed look.

"I can't leave," the man protested. He was dwarven with an elaborately braided beard. "I've told you, contact Berghold. I'm not a citizen of Heffog and may not be taken as a slave—"

The merchant made a gesture. A guard stepped forward and hauled the protestor away. The dwarf began to yell and horror dawned in his eyes. He had believed until that moment that he might somehow get out of this. Finally, he had realized he would not.

The other slaves were guided away. Any who resisted were struck with staves or fists. A few of them had clenched their jaws and tried not to resist and make it worse for themselves. Ben watched them go while his blood pressure rose. His hands were clamped behind his back as he tried to fight the urge to run after them. He wanted to haul every one of them out of this place.

A swift kick to his ankle reminded him of where he was. Elantria stepped forward to speak to Jorys, all smiles and quiet competence, while her two companions waited in the shadows.

The man looked at them only casually and shrugged. He and Elantria exchanged a few more words before she nodded to Orien to take his break first. The elf would take a roundabout path to the kitchens, he knew, although not conspicuously so, and he would begin to chart not only the lower part of the house but also the movement of the servants and guards.

That had always been the plan, but Ben had the distinct impression that she was also keeping him close so he didn't run off and do something like free the slaves. She was worried.

Well, she should be worried. He wanted to throw up at the thought of the people being hauled off to the slave market at that very moment. She said she was realistic about what she could achieve and that she wanted slow results, but every day the system didn't change, she consigned people to death and slavery.

Ben made his way through the day quietly and without much incident. Jorys was well guarded, so no one would try to break into his house to murder him. It meant that all he needed to do was drift around after him and not fidget too much.

He was given a brief break to eat dinner, seated on a stool in the corner of the kitchen, and it was only a couple of hours later that Orien came to join him. "He wants to discuss our trial run."

That was the signal. It meant that Elantria or Orien had successfully cracked the vault and incapacitated the guards inside and that they needed help to get the gold out to the waiting carriage.

Even after the absolute horror show of a day—he had spent most of it fantasizing about brutal ways to kill Jorys—he had to admit he was excited at helping with a heist. It was unexpectedly fun to find himself in the middle of one, especially since he'd always enjoyed heist movies.

He simply hadn't ever expected to think, while in the midst of stealing countless riches, that the world might be better served by him assassinating the person he attempted to rob.

Orien led him to the vault and Ben took a heavy chest of gold coins and hurried up the stairs to the waiting carriage. This part of the house seemed to be entirely deserted, but his co-conspirators were both insistent that he move silently.

A few minutes later, he realized why. As he returned inside from the carriage and headed to the vault, he looked down a corridor to see none other than Jorys. The merchant was seated at his desk, working.

And he was completely ignorant of the fact that, if he turned, he would have a clear line of sight to the people robbing him.

The sheer balls it took to plan the heist this way distracted Ben for a moment, but close on the heels of his admiration came another emotion—hatred. Jorys was there and, it seemed, unattended. There was no reason to choose between robbing him and assassinating him.

He saw Orien gesture out of the corner of his eye and motion for him to hurry, but he wasn't paying attention anymore.

His focus fixed on his target, he ran toward Jorys as he drew his dagger.

CHAPTER FIFTEEN

He had something of a head start. Elantria and Orien were still a flight of stairs away, coming out of the vault.

If he were honest, however, Ben would have to admit that he hadn't thought about that. He merely ran and no longer even tried to be quiet. This was purely reflexive, and he hadn't chosen his moment or hoped to prevent them from interfering.

His survival instinct tried to remind him that he didn't even know if there was another guard in the room. There probably was.

In moments, he pushed through the door and there was nothing to be done except face what awaited him. He surged into Jorys's study with his dagger drawn and it was damned clear what his intention was. The merchant turned in his seat, but Ben wasn't looking at him.

Yes, there was another guard here—and, worse, it was the gigantic man they had seen at the front door that morning.

Ben watched as the man whipped his arm around, drew a knife, and flipped it to hold it by the blade and he threw himself onto the floor. The weapon whistled over his head and embedded itself in the open door. He looked at it and had a moment of paralysis. It was too late to think of the might-have-been. If he had given into paralysis a moment before, he would be dead now.

Still, he couldn't afford to be paralyzed now either. The guard lunged across the room with a roar and he pushed to his feet and dove sideways into the hallway. His momentum carried him down the half-flight of stairs that led to the study. He grasped the banister and curled into a ball while the guard followed him out.

There wasn't time for anything except an attack. Ben had never been in a one-on-one fight with an assassin before, but he knew that turning his back and running would doom him, and every instinct fell in line to help. He uncoiled as his adversary came down the stairs. His head was averted, which left a gap at his shoulder for a tackle. When his shoulder met the area above the guard's knees, he drove up with all his might.

It didn't take as much force as he expected. He was, after all, only slightly modifying the guard's trajectory. He looked up in surprise as the legs flipped over his head and the man thudded heavily on his back.

He could hear Orien and Elantria and hoped they would help him because right now was the best opening he would get. As he sprinted up the stairs, he ignored the sound of someone hissing his name and ran after Jorys.

Ben caught the man on the other side of the room. The merchant was trying to escape, oblivious to the sacrifice his guard was making. That was, of course, the point of a bodyguard, but he was so contemptuous of his target that he would hold it against him anyway.

When he grasped his quarry's arm and dragged him around, he took a punch full in the face. He staggered back and stars burst across his vision. Determined to not lose the opportunity, he thrust his knife forward as hard as he could and he struck something. The blade encountered resistance and a scream followed.

When his vision cleared, he saw his knife plunged into Jorys' left shoulder. He yanked it out and felt a wave of instant revulsion. Despite his abhorrence of violence, he was killing someone. The resistance against his knife was bone and flesh and he would have to stab again.

He shoved the revulsion away. Two weeks before, he had made a mistake. He hadn't been willing to use violence when it might have prevented who knew how many deaths. Every day the merchant was alive, he would sell slaves and hurt the people of his district.

He had to die.

Ben thrust the knife again, this time into Jorys' chest. The man wheezed. He was dying and he knew it—the sheer amount of blood from the first stab wound had already doomed him, and this merely hastened the end.

A commotion erupted behind him, but he didn't care.

"Who…*are* you?" Jorys rasped.

"Someone who won't let you get away with this anymore," he told him, his voice low. "Today, you sent ten people to a life of slavery. Who knows how many you have doomed? You should feel lucky you only have one life to lose in return."

The merchant collapsed and died at his feet, and he fought the urge to throw up everywhere. He heard footsteps behind him and he was so disoriented that he almost didn't care if it was Elantria or the guard.

Then he realized that if it was the guard, his companions might be in trouble, and he spun toward the sound.

He had never seen her looking this angry. Of course, he hadn't known her very long, but he had seen her fight for her life and speak to enemies, and the look on her face now was chilling. She looked at him like she wanted to kill him.

"Come on," she said, her voice clipped. She caught him by the arm and yanked him out of the room.

Without protest, he stumbled past the body of the guard and out into the night. Orien was huddled in the carriage and held a hand over a shallow but bloody wound on his arm. He watched as Elantria pushed the other man into the cab. Ben met his gaze and felt a sudden wave of guilt but there was no expression at all in the elf's eyes.

The carriage lurched into motion. The wheels were wrapped in cloth, as were the horse's hooves, and a heavy fog all around them felt somehow magical. He had no doubt that she had chosen both magic and technology to make her getaway.

They were a few streets away before she spoke.

"What the *hell* was that?" She did not look at him and that, for some reason, showed him how angry she was.

"I told you I made mistakes," he said passionately. "I told you I didn't stop someone who wanted to commit murder and because of that, she brought an army to attack the fae. Their wells of magic were destroyed, their king was almost killed, and hundreds died, if not more, defending the castle that day. I *told* you I wouldn't make the same mistake again—"

"And *Orien* told you that you might make it worse for people if you charged in and tried to bring justice!" Elantria snapped. "He warned you that you didn't know what you were doing. *I* warned you, and you didn't listen!"

"You were simply going to let him keep selling slaves!" he roared.

"I know that I am one person who cannot possibly stand in the way of the entire slave trade!" she retorted. "And keep your voice down. This carriage is magicked, but it's not infallible."

"All you fucking care about is your tiny jobs," he whispered angrily. "You keep telling yourself you can't make any big changes so you pull off little heists like this to salve your conscience."

He honestly thought she would hit him. Her fingers twitched

and curled into a fist and her face was a picture. She stared at him with such hatred in her eyes that he felt cold all the way through.

"Do you think you stopped the slave trade with this?" she asked finally. "Do you think because one slave trader was killed in his house that you've fixed everything?"

"Maybe other people will think twice before—"

"Do you know who will take over for Jorys in that district?" Elantria demanded.

Dread settled in and he swallowed. "No. Who?"

"It's one of three people," she said, her voice clipped. "If he had passed naturally, he would have designated an heir and there would have been a *chance* of someone else taking power without a fight. Now, you've all but assured a war of succession. His son will fight his two top lieutenants and every one of them is *worse* than Jorys was." She all but hissed the last words at him in utter fury.

Ben stared silently at her.

"You haven't taken that district out of the control of a warlord," she told him in utter contempt, "and you haven't stopped the slave trade. If nothing else, you've taken one of the sellers out of the market, which only makes slave-trading more profitable for the rest of them. You've doomed the people of Jorys' district to a violent crackdown and an unwinnable game of trying to play loyal to whoever they think will win his position." Quietly, she added, "And you've almost certainly doomed any chance we had of helping there again."

He looked away. Now that the assassination was over and the adrenaline began to fade, there was only the sick, nauseated certainty that he had done something terribly wrong. He had made things worse by trying to do the right thing.

No. He straightened in his seat. Maybe there was a larger change that needed to happen, but he wouldn't be the kind of person who slunk around in the shadows and said that justice couldn't be delivered because there might be fallout.

Jorys had brought this on himself, and he would kill anyone who tried to take his place. He would free that district and then he would turn and ask Elantria why she had aimed so low.

Because she was part of this city. She had wanted him for this.

"You wanted someone to do the things you wouldn't dare do," he told her. "You wanted the new perspective. You were raised by the elites of this city."

"Which means I know far, far better than you the constraints and ramifications of acting against them," she told him furiously. "I know how many ways they use to prop themselves up and I know what we're up against if we try to dislodge them."

"You wanted me to think differently than you," he retorted. "You *are* a revolutionary and you *know* you've been pulling your punches too much and let people get away with murder and slavery and God knows what else. You're ashamed of your cowardice and—"

"You know *nothing* about me," Elantria snapped. "Nothing." She pounded on the top of the carriage and it lurched to a stop and almost threw him into Orien's lap. Before either of them could say anything, she pushed the door open. "Get out," she told Ben.

He stared at her.

"Get out," she repeated. She met his gaze with one of cold fury and leaned back. He gathered his composure and climbed out of the carriage.

Once outside, he began to strip his armor and weapons off. He wouldn't keep anything of hers if she threw him out into the city.

She shook her head, though, reached into a hidden coin purse, and withdrew three copper coins, which she tossed at him. Her face was blank. "I'll not have your death on my conscience," she said quietly. "But if you're willing to kill and sow chaos that will spill over onto my people, neither will I protect you. Get out of my sight. Zaara and Kural's trust in you was misplaced."

Ben met Orien's eyes for one instant before the carriage door slammed shut again. The elf still looked completely expressionless, his fingers clutching the bloody wound on his arm.

The carriage rumbled away and he was left standing in the fading mist, alone in the dark of the night.

CHAPTER SIXTEEN

The twins had fallen asleep in cozy tents with beds that were the softest they had ever slept in, fluffy blankets that were somehow not too hot, and pajamas that felt like silk. With the chirps of the birds and the insects and the comfort of being close to one another again, both of them had drifted to sleep in record time.

And, Prima reflected, she probably should not be surprised that it was ten AM and they were both still asleep. They were teenagers and she had gone out of her way to make sure they were as comfortable as possible.

Eventually, she gave up on trying to be subtle and gradually changed the fabric of the tents to allow progressively more light in. It took the better part of an hour, but she did finally stir the two of them to stumble around and make vague noises of complaint.

They both tried to go back to sleep, of course, but that was handily taken care of when she winked the beds out of existence and Taigan was so sleepy that she forgot she could summon things.

Once they were up and eating breakfast, the AI bided her time for a while. After all, she had enough to check in on. Half a world away, Ben tried to find somewhere to hide out after he'd assassinated someone.

Prima had genuinely not seen that coming. It worried her a little how quickly he had shifted from refusing to kill anyone to viewing assassination as a tool that was not only allowed but morally essential.

She watched him for a while—he displayed far more judgment when it came to selecting a hiding place than he had when it came to perpetrating a con—but kept an eye on the twins so she could see when they had finished breakfast.

Both had the kind of metabolisms that mimicked a squirrel on a high dose of cocaine. She watched as Taigan ate an entire plate of scrambled eggs, Jamie downed three plate-sized pancakes smothered in syrup, each of them ate easily an entire pig's worth of bacon, and together, polished off over two loaves' worth of toast.

When they leaned back with their hands over their stomachs, she decided it was time to get them moving.

"Good morning."

The young people jumped.

"Your journey begins this morning," Prima told them. *"Normally, one seeks something that is far away, but on your journey, you will be side by side. You will, together, seek each other out. Are you ready?"*

Taigan nodded at once. Jamie downed an entire mug of coffee before he did the same.

"We will set out whenever you are ready," she told them.

To her surprise and amusement, both immediately set about packing up the camp. Being all-powerful, she had simply created everything in it from nothing and had been prepared to do the reverse as well. It was pleasant, however, to see them make their beds and tidy everything.

While they did that, she rigged floating whiteboards that would automatically write the things they said if they spoke to one another. Then, dressed in loose clothing and huge camping boots, they set off in the direction she indicated with a breeze and a cluster of sparkles.

"So, where are we going?" Taigan asked her.

"Today, you will climb Aryoka Mountain," she told them. Ahead of the twins, the mists cleared and the mountain came into view. It wasn't massive but it would certainly take at least half a day to reach the summit.

"Did you see that before?" Jamie asked his sister. The whiteboards she'd prepared worked extremely well as his words appeared seconds later. "Because I think it simply…appeared."

"That does sound like Prima."

"What? She moves mountains around?"

"Ask her yourself," Taigan said with a shrug. "I know I would if I had all that magic."

"Prima? Did you make that mountain from nothing, or did I, uh…you know, miss a massive mountain?"

"You can *be quite oblivious,"* Prima said wickedly. *"But relax. It's not covered in jackalopes."*

Jamie, who'd had a bad run-in with jackalopes during his first visit to the game, grumbled something under his breath.

They started up the slope together. Prima had made a path… barely. There was a route—nothing as cruel as a path that wound into a cliff and required backtracking—but it was far from easy to traverse.

"Prima," Taigan panted as she struggled up a series of too-high steps, "what exactly are we looking for at the top of the mountain?"

"There is a temple," she replied. *"Inside is a pool of water that legend says will show you your deepest desire."*

Both twins stopped in their tracks.

"Wait, seriously?" the girl asked.

"That's so lame," Jamie blurted. They each nodded at what was on the other's whiteboard.

Prima, who had structured this exercise with particular pitfalls in mind, bristled nonetheless.

"I, uh…" He scratched his head. "I'm not sure I want to see my deepest desire while sitting next to one of my sisters. *She* won't see it, will she?"

"*Ew*," Taigan said. She hadn't thought along the same lines and this was an unwelcome revelation to her. "Wait, seriously? Your deepest desire isn't something like going to Mars, it's—I mean, your *deepest* desire, out of *all* your desires…just *ew*."

"Don't judge," Jamie said defensively. "And I worked statistically. Like, the thing I think about most often."

"Ew!" She flailed her arms. "No! Wrong! Stop!"

"Would you like a spray bottle?"

"Yes! *Please!*"

Prima snickered. To them, she said, *"You can see very few things the other does in the world so I would be very surprised if you could see each other's dreams in the pool. However, as you hike, you might want to think about what you expect to see."*

"Why?" Taigan asked. "If it will show us what our heart's desire is, why spend time thinking about it now?"

If the AI had hair, she would tear it out right now. She began to understand why humans ran off to become hermits. It was because the rest of them were so completely ridiculous.

"Climb the damned mountain."

Two sets of eyebrows shot up. They looked instinctively at each other—a few feet apart and unable to see one another—but it was one of those little moments that both gave her hope. And filled her with fear.

These two had known each other since before they were born and looked to each other when they processed the world. They bickered good-naturedly about anything and everything—more things than most people ever could bicker about because they understood so much more about each other than others did.

She regretted snapping at them, but they set about climbing the mountain with goodwill.

"I genuinely," Taigan all but growled as she hauled herself up an embankment, "have zero idea what I'll see in there."

"Me, neither." Jamie studied a gap, considered it for a moment, and leapt. He made the distance but banged his shin on landing. "Ow! Hell. I'm okay."

"Are you bleeding?" she asked.

"Nah." He was and bright red blood trickled down his shin, but it wasn't much. When he looked at Prima and put a finger to his lips, she responded with a sigh only he could hear.

"Wait," his sister said. She had found something rather like stairs and she now climbed them with determination. "You *don't* know what you'll see?"

"Now that you've pointed out that it could be anything, that broadens the…category…thingy."

"Good Lord." Taigan rolled her eyes. "Okay, Prima, tell me it's close."

"It's a mountain."

Both twins made a whimpering noise.

"Don't make me get the jackalopes."

"Oh, fuck," Jamie said. "Climb, climb, climb!"

"Jackalopes aren't real, are they?" his sister asked. She hadn't shaken the habit yet of looking for him when she spoke, and Prima hoped she could get the two of them to see each other before it became natural for them to talk this way.

He was more task-focused and Prima had only seen Taigan like that when she was running. Currently, he took a side route around a boulder. It was by far the more difficult way to go but he hadn't checked to see if the other way would be easier. She watched in amusement as he jumped and pushed himself up. "They're real," he said. "And they're *mean*, and they're *not* the size of normal bunnies!"

"Like, cow-sized or very *small*?" The girl raised one eyebrow.

"I'm picturing be swarmed by scorpions, only it's tiny, angry bunnies."

Jamie laughed at that. "No, I meant big. Not cow-sized, but *big*. Think…chest high? And the *teeth*. Emmy and I fought some."

"*Emmy* is here?" Taigan stopped dead. Her hands were scuffed and dirty and had left a few smudges across her face where she had wiped the sweat away and tucked stray wisps of hair behind her ears. "Is she with you?"

"No. This time, it's only me."

"*This* time?"

"We both went in to test it when Mom and Dad came to see the facility. They weren't quite sure they wanted to hook you up to it and the team offered to let us try it. I don't think either of them did, only me and Emmy."

She kept climbing. Her face was sad now and her movements jerky.

"Sis?"

Taigan didn't respond right away. Tears glistened in her eyes and she sniffed at regular intervals. She climbed with single-minded intensity now.

Jamie could only see her by the whiteboard that hovered nearby and he hurried to catch up. He seemed stronger than his sister, but she had a head-start and she wasn't paying attention to pain or tiredness right now.

"Tell me you're okay," he called.

"Of course I'm not okay!" The words exploded out of her and she looked furiously in his direction. One tear had escaped. "That's why you're *here*, remember?"

"Okay, but what did I say?"

"I hate this part!" She began to cry and her voice had a raw edge to it. "Hearing about all the things I missed while I was under, hearing about all of you making decisions—about *me*—only I'm not there, this not even being *our* thing because it was your and Emmy's first, and now I'm only—" She brushed angrily at her hair to get it out of her face. "An afterthought," she said.

"Everything is set up around you!" he responded sharply. "How the hell could you be an afterthought? You were why we were *there*!"

"Yeah, but you were there only the four of you!" Taigan shouted. She climbed so fast now that she constantly missed holds, slipped, and gritted her teeth on exclamations of pain. Each only made her angrier and it would be logical to stop, but she wouldn't. Prima looked on with concern.

She had set this up to make them talk but she hadn't envisioned it going like *this*.

Taigan pushed onto a gently sloping stretch of rock and shale. She looked at the temple, then down to where Jamie was.

"You know," she said, almost too quietly for him to hear, "the four real members of the family. And then me. The one you can't count on."

He stopped and fixed his gaze on where he thought she was. "We never forget you."

"I know." Her lip trembled. "But there's a difference between being someone people think about and being someone who's *there*." Quietly, she added, "I'm not angry at you, Jamie. Not at any of you. But it sucks to have this catch-up talk every time I wake up—what everyone did while I lay in a hospital bed. And this time, it feels more personal—like you and Emmy got into the game and had fun together, and you and I can't even *see* each other."

The terrible thing about human thought patterns, Prima realized, wasn't that they were so illogical or that they made so many jumps—it was how much sense they made after the fact. It was the way you could say something that was simply a fact but it would hurt someone more than a punch to the face. After you'd done it, you could see what you'd done but at the time, the possibility didn't even occur to you.

Jamie climbed up the same rock Taigan had used and the two of them stood together, almost in the same place. They were overlapping and the girl sometimes disappeared entirely into his larger frame.

"We'll fix this," he said, and his voice shook with conviction. "I know it's worst for you, but—"

"I'm usually asleep for it," she interrupted. "So it's probably worse for you."

"You know what I mean. This…whatever it is. Glitch. We'll fix it. Don't think of us doing things without you. Think of us finding new ways to bring you home. We aren't whole without you."

Taigan leaned her head on his shoulder—or would have if she hadn't been halfway through his body.

"Let's go see the temple," she said. "I'll only see me living a normal day, and I hope like hell I won't see yours."

He laughed and the two of them set off together.

CHAPTER SEVENTEEN

Ben had no idea where the hell he was going.

He tried to keep his mind blank. When he thought about what had happened, he was furious, but guilt and shame waited offstage. He never let them into his thoughts but he knew they were there. They were waiting for their moment to strike.

It wasn't until he was a few streets away that he realized why it all felt so familiar. It shouldn't be, in all honesty. He had never assassinated someone and been thrown out by his crime-boss protector in the middle of the night.

But he *had* done what someone told him specifically not to do, only for the whole situation to go up in flames. After which he always—always—ran away. He picked up and headed to a new job, new relationship, or new remote village. Each time he did that, he told himself that this was why he didn't want to settle down. People were simply too ridiculous.

And, the whole time, he wouldn't let a part of him speak because it insisted that he knew this was his fault—that *he* was the constant. He approached every new job with hope but that grew slimmer every time. There was always the pit of certainty in his stomach that this would be exactly like the last time.

Of course it would. He was the problem and he couldn't leave himself behind.

Now, he wanted to cringe at the memories of climbing mountains alone, staring at sunrises, meditating. and giving up his possessions. It turned out that you could do all the things that were supposed to give you clarity, but it was possible to do every one of them in bad faith.

He put his head down and darted glances to his left and his right as he walked. Sometimes, people would come to the ends of the alleyways or the shadowed windows to watch as he passed. Heffog was scarcely quieter at night, only more watchful.

The itching feeling at the back of his neck ebbed and flowed as he passed through neighborhoods. Who could say what it was —what tiny sounds or glimpses of movement the body saw but the mind couldn't catch—but you could tell when you were somewhere unsafe.

Ben merely didn't know *how* unsafe.

The sensation unsettled him constantly and he made a decision. The next time he was somewhere he wasn't as afraid and there weren't as many watchful eyes, he would look for a place to hide.

Time blurred and he wasn't sure how long it had been before he found it. The sky was still black, but there was enough light from distant lanterns and streetlights that he could see the buildings around him. He crept up to one of them and looked in the window. The opening gaped in the wall, uncovered. His careful study showed the remains of a cloth window covering tied out of the way and now more rags and thread than actual cloth.

He couldn't see anyone inside or hear the small noises of stirring or snoring, but he wasn't foolish enough to walk into an empty building in the middle of the night.

A different idea crept in and was one he could focus on with a greater degree of confidence.

This building, like many in the area, had been made with

plaster daubed hastily over wood and stone, along with a few mud bricks. No one had protected the bricks properly from the elements and they had worn away beneath the outer layer. It wasn't a fantastic set of holds and not the kind of thing you climbed if you made smart decisions.

But he wasn't making smart decisions right now, and there was something to be said for choosing the best of the bad decisions available to you.

He sighted up the side of the building. Doing a flash—a one-track climb with no false starts—didn't seem very likely there, but he didn't want to take any longer than he had to. Experience had taught him that a few minutes spent planning his route meant far less time climbing—and far less chance of bad falls.

The blue sky and the falling feeling were back in the pit of his stomach and he leaned forward and tried not to gag. The last thing he needed was to attract attention.

All he wanted was to forget falling—and seeing Mike fall.

"Ben, are you all right? Your heart rate spiked."

Ben didn't answer for a moment. "I was…thinking of the accident."

He got the sense of Prima nodding. *"Tell me if I can help,"* she said finally.

That made him smile. "I will. Thank you. Now, hold my beer."

"I have no hands—wait, beer? You don't have beer."

"It's an expression one says when one is about to do something stupid."

"Then why haven't I heard it from you before? Zing!"

For a moment, he had to lean against the wall and muffle his laughter with his hand. This day had been a nightmare and he was very sure his laughter was about more than the particular joke, but an AI poking fun at him was legitimately as funny as all hell. It took several minutes for him to calm, during which time he was convinced several times that he would break a rib.

When he was relatively sure he wouldn't burst out laughing

again, he began to climb. The handholds were rough and he collected more splinters than he knew what to do with, but he couldn't focus on that right now.

He used the corner of the building as his main route. It was the roughest part of the building with stone blocks and pieces of wooden planks. There were occasional easy holds where mud bricks had crumbled away, although not as many as he'd like.

On the other hand, he would like the building to stay up once he got to the top.

This was easier than his first couple of climbs. He seemed to be re-learning the way pressure felt on his fingertips and how to balance on the edge of a foot. Sometimes, he forgot that this was more difficult now and at others, it seemed to come naturally. His weight was braced on his feet and his fingers only lightly brushed the stone when he was at rest.

Moving from the corner up and over the roof was undignified, not to mention risky. Ben had not been able to determine the composition of the roof and his hands traced over ceramic tiles while he hung there, rather like a desperate sloth. He needed to shift his feet off the edge of the building to swing back so he could haul himself up.

It was simply that he couldn't seem to make his feet do it. It wasn't that his body couldn't tell where they were but that his brain demanded loudly to know why he was thirty-odd feet above the ground and why he wanted to go even higher. His frontal lobe wanted him to know, in no uncertain terms, that this was a foolish idea and he should go down immediately.

He would have to do it somehow, so exhaled a long breath and made his mind a blank. Cautiously, he unhooked one foot and moved the leg back, then the second one. His body didn't swing wildly—he had enough core strength, especially in this world—but he was acutely aware of the dangers of being this high up.

Once, that had been a thrill. After the accident, it was more complicated.

Hiking himself up over the edge was more difficult than he had anticipated. Unlike a wall, he couldn't push out with his feet and use the momentum of tethered arms to swing up. This was all core and upper body and relied on his newly restored and still faulty hands.

Yeah, this wasn't his brightest idea ever.

Finally, he accomplished it by swinging his right leg up and pushing with the extra hold. The roof edge, thankfully, was curved in like a pagoda, which meant he could get his feet under him more easily and rest for a moment. He sat and leaned back against the upper part of the curve while his heart hammered and sweat cooled on his skin.

When he moved to turn, his relief fled. It was the result of only the slightest give under his feet but enough to make his breath catch in his throat. His heart seized and he saw the blue again and felt the tumble. But when the spots cleared from his vision, he wasn't falling and the little clatter he'd heard was gone. He was still safe.

Ceramic shattered on paving stones. He froze again and his heart made a concerted effort to leap sideways out of his body.

Ben waited for ten breaths, then twenty, listening for the sound of footsteps or creaking shutters, but heard nothing. Finally, he took two steps and hauled himself over the final level of the roof with single-minded determination. As his first climbing instructor had said, "Tell your body what to do and then get your mind out of the way."

He stood on a fairly wide, flat roof, recessed by two feet or so. Someone had lived there once but not recently, and anything of value had long since been stripped. There was only the faint detritus left after a move and after rain and wind had swept most of the rest away. He could see a scrap of a rag, the remains of an old flag, and pieces of string hanging from some tiles. Four holes in the floor suggested that a covering of some kind had been held up with poles.

While he didn't have any of that, what he did have was a place where no one else seemed to be. He'd take it.

With a heavy sigh, he sat and let his arms fall at his sides. Now that he was over the edge of the roof, every muscle seemed to tremble.

"I fucked up, didn't I?"

Silence was not what he hoped to hear.

"Prima?"

"You didn't seem like you were quite done with your part of the conversation yet."

Ben cursed internally at the AI for being astute. He didn't like that. She had a point, though. "I wasn't. I don't think I *did* fuck up."

"There it is."

"There what is? She's getting on my case, but she's copping out on this whole thing. 'One person can't stand in the way of the slave trade.'" He made finger quotes bitterly. If anyone was watching, he would probably have looked completely insane when he mouthed words almost silently and gestured. "They won't change because someone asks them nicely and lays out a gold road. They'll stop because it gets too difficult to keep doing business, and that isn't *pleasant.* Does she think she's teaching them a *lesson* by stealing their money? It goes back into the community so they can suck it out again. That's a stupid system."

"Mmm, rain and droughts work much the same way."

"Whose side are you on?" Ben demanded.

"I'm not on anyone's side. I'm an observer."

"Kind of." He scowled at the sky, which had begun to show the first hint of dawn. "I'm only saying you don't stop something like this by turning away and pretending not to see it."

Prima said nothing.

"Well? *Do* you?"

"I think," she said after a short hesitation, *"that if there were an easy, assured route for this kind of thing, slavery would not still exist."*

"I didn't say it would be easy," he snapped in response.

"Yes, but that's the issue, isn't it? It's never merely inconvenient. It makes you give up things you aren't prepared to give."

With that, she gave every indication of withdrawing respectfully from the conversation and left him to stare into the middle distance. Finally, as the sky lightened, he managed to fall into a fitful sleep.

It had been a long night.

CHAPTER EIGHTEEN

The twins walked into the temple, each with their hand outstretched, reaching for contact.

Prima found it fascinating how much living creatures relied on their sense of touch for comfort. It had been built into the algorithms governing how characters interacted, and she had initially discounted it. As she understood it, physical contact was for romantic purposes and was used sporadically for friendship and other social interactions.

Now, she began to think that without a body of her own, she had misunderstood something fundamental.

The pool was positioned at the end of the temple. Mindful of the information she had researched on architecture and human psychology, she had made the environment as comforting as she could with muted, fairly even lighting and a low ceiling that slanted down at the corners. Although sky and clouds could be seen outside, she hoped the twins felt safe there.

Their heart rates *were* slowing. Prima gave herself some congratulations.

They reached the pool and each looked to where the other

would be. They couldn't see each other's faces, which meant they couldn't decide by tiny flickers and gestures who should go first.

"Do you want to go?" Jamie asked. "Or should I?"

Taigan hesitated. The AI got the sense that making this decision through words was difficult for her. "You go first," she said finally.

Jamie approached the pool. It was wide, paved with tiles of various pale blues, and fed by a little fountain so the water barely moved.

She would see now if she'd gambled well on human psychology. It seemed she wasn't very good at this, and after a few missteps in the past weeks, she began to worry that she would never grasp what was required.

He knelt and stared at his reflection, bit his lip, and looked to where Taigan hung back.

"Oh, come on. You probably won't see it and it won't be gross."

His sister laughed slightly and crept closer. She joined him in looking at the water and her face fell when she couldn't see their two reflections together.

Jamie stared, waited, and eventually, extended his hand tentatively to touch the surface. He held back at first as if worried that a curse would come out of nowhere and drag him into the underworld, but nothing happened when he touched it. He only saw exactly what Prima wanted him to see—his face and nothing more.

"Prima, am I supposed to do something?" he asked finally.

"I can only tell you what the legend is."

"But you wouldn't have hauled us up here if it didn't work, right? Right? Prima?" He looked around and his tone changed. "But how *could* it work? How could a game see…"

He was getting too close to the truth.

"See if Taigan can make it work."

"Oh. Good point." He looked in the girl's direction, distracted from his thoughts. "You give it a go. If we're existing differently, then maybe you'll be able to do it."

"Maybe." Taigan sounded doubtful. "I simply look into it?"

"Don't ask me. I couldn't make it work."

"Good point." She knelt and there was a moment where her frame and her brother's melded. He stood and stepped back.

She closed her eyes for a moment while she propped herself on her hands and thought hard, then opened her eyes and looked down. Her reflection mirrored her frown and she waited with admirable patience for a picture to appear. When it didn't, she sighed, closed her eyes, and opened them to try again.

This was part of the plan, but it was surprisingly difficult to keep quiet while they worked toward the conclusion. Prima distracted herself with plotting a three-body problem while Taigan tried her best to make the pool work.

Finally, however, the girl blew a breath out. "Okay, I can't do it, either."

"Well, shit." Jamie knelt nearby. "Prima, did you consider that we might merely be stupid?"

"You are humans. Sorry, low blow."

"Yeah, funny." He looked up. "Remember when you didn't understand how language worked and convinced me that my sister was dead?"

"Point taken."

"Uh-huh." He sat and crossed his legs.

"Maybe it was meant to be paired with prayer," she suggested as casually as she could. *"After all, this is a temple. Perhaps some...meditation?"*

"You really don't know?" Taigan asked suspiciously.

"A great deal of the lore was already here when I came to the game."

It was a specious excuse at best, but they both accepted it with a shrug. Prima couldn't decide if that made them stupid or if it made her an asshole.

"Shall we try meditation?" the girl asked Jamie.

"I don't know. This is getting a little 'Oracle of Delphi.'"

"What does *that* mean?"

"You know, where people would bring gifts and she'd burn them and inhale the chemicals and do an acid trip and tell them about it? Like, it wasn't anything real. It was only hallucinogens."

"You take the fun out of *everything*." Taigan sat with a thump and rolled her eyes before she closed them.

He had enough of a sense about his sister to sit with her and also try to meditate. Whatever was going through their heads—and Prima couldn't see *that*, however much she wanted to—their faces moved sometimes with shadows of emotion, but they both seemed determined to make the pool work.

She truly was an asshole. While she did it for a good reason, playing tricks on people didn't feel right. She had never done something like this before, but she had heard the PIVOT team members discussing meditation and she had done research of her own. Meditation skills, honed over time, allowed the user to move through states of consciousness at will.

And something seemed to be working. With interest and hope, she watched as the two of them started to flicker into the same way of being.

It was working.

Prima focused intently to make sure she hadn't misinterpreted what she'd seen. It was *working*. They had their eyes closed, but it was *working*.

She wanted to give a whoop but noticed something unfortunate.

Taigan didn't flicker into Jamie's way of being. It was the other way around. He began to go into her state. The AI panicked and dropped something loudly to scare the two of them. She should do this with less guesswork and panic, but she didn't have time to think—all she wanted was to pull Jamie out of this immediately.

As both twins jumped and swore, there was a split-second

where Taigan flickered into her brother's space. It was only for a moment, but his sudden, sharp look was enough to tell Prima that it hadn't been a trick of the algorithms.

That gave her an idea.

"Prima?" Taigan called.

"Something is coming," she said. *"In both your realities."*

"Shitshitshitshitshit," Jamie muttered. "Taigan, are you okay? Taigan!"

The girl darted a glance at his whiteboard. "I'm fine. For now." She swallowed. "I'm—"

Prima knew the sentence was supposed to end with scared, but Taigan didn't want to worry her brother. The AI tried to calm herself and wait. If this worked, her instincts and theories would be vindicated.

Well, she would know soon enough if it would work.

The jackalopes burst out of the brush at the edges of the temple, one on either side. The young people only seemed to see one apiece, which was good. The creatures snarled as they bounded toward the twins, their fur glistening and teeth gleaming.

Please let this work, please let this work, please let this work... Thankfully, the AI hadn't projected that as her version of a verbal statement.

Taigan launched forward with a yell directly toward her jack-alope. There was a moment of confusion while Jamie saw her and his jackalope did too. The animal skidded to a halt and tried to choose a target, but he lunged at it with a noise halfway between a yodel and a shriek.

Prima made a mental note to tease him relentlessly about that later.

Physical danger was shifting Taigan into the same level of consciousness. Now that they had done the work to make her aware of her body, she had begun to get the hang of *being* again.

The AI surged happily but stopped hastily so she wouldn't over-load her servers.

Hopefully, no one on the PIVOT team had seen the processing flare. Humans could be quite oblivious, but they also had a habit of noticing things you didn't want them to.

Due to her freakish speed and the others' distraction, Taigan reached her jackalope first. She didn't seem to have a plan—something Prima was distressingly familiar with after watching Justin, Ben, and Dotty—but she was also prepared to do anything and everything to win the fight.

She started by grasping the jackalope by the horns and wrenching it sideways.

The creature did not know what to do with this particular strategy. It was too well-grounded to simply flop over, but it didn't have a long enough snout to bite her or long enough limbs to scratch her. The two combatants circled, locked in their standoff.

Jamie still had his sword. He uttered another yodel and slashed at his adversary, which leapt back with a hiss. Blood stained its flanks.

"Do you want a piece of this?" he taunted. "Huh? Don't you dare hurt my fucking sister. I'll kill you."

"I don't think jackalopes speak English."

"They understand tone!" he shouted in response and swung the weapon again.

Taigan shifted her feet a few times as if testing a theory, then kicked her opponent squarely in the chest. Its teeth snapped but gained no purchase, given the angle of her leg. She still yelped and withdrew the limb, then stumbled, having lost sight of the animal for a second.

It looked equally confused.

She flickered back and the two of them shrieked and charged each other again. Taigan dived sideways, flickered out, and rolled to her feet in time to catch the jackalope's antlers again. This time, as she held on and swung her leg—aiming precisely for the mouth with her knee—she flickered out for good. The creature hurtled through the space where she had been and skidded out the side of the temple, and she whirled as Jamie stabbed his opponent through the mouth.

Reflexively, she clapped her hands over her mouth. The animal slumped and her brother yanked his sword out before he saw her out of the corner of his eye.

"Taigan?" He sounded like he might cry.

They stared in shock and hope, shaking, before they ran to each other and collided in a tangle of limbs and heads and black hair. Prima couldn't tell if what she heard was laughter or crying. They wrapped their arms around each other and hung on for dear life.

At some point, the laughter stopped and the sound became crying. Both shuddered with sobs, a breakdown that made her the saddest she had been since—well, since Dotty.

Sadness was much like happiness, she decided. It was the urge to do something or process something, but there was nothing to do except exist while the emotion ran through one's system. She didn't think she liked it, but something about this situation made her want to explode, she was so full of joy.

Joy, but not happiness.

Emotions were *weird.*

"What the hell?" Taigan choked finally. "You have a *sword*? I didn't have a sword."

Jamie started to laugh. He laughed until he was crying again as he held her. "You're here," he whispered. "You're here. I can see you. You're here."

"I'm here." She squeezed her arms around him. "I want to see Emmy and Mom and Dad too."

"You can. Of course you can. We'll get them here." He drew back and looked at her. "Taigan, when I thought about what I wanted most—"

He stopped. She had flickered out again into her separate existence.

"Dammit!" both twins said at the same time. The words appeared on their respective whiteboards.

Then, at the same time, they added, "It doesn't matter."

"We can do it again," Taigan affirmed.

"We can do it again," he echoed.

"You can do it again," Prima agreed.

CHAPTER NINETEEN

Ben woke when a shadow fell across him. He sat with a snort and his limbs flailed, and he grimaced when he realized he was both tormented by aching muscles and *far* too hot. His mouth felt like sandpaper. When he saw what had cast the shadow, he scrambled back across the roof and felt for his knife.

The woman smiled at him. Her blonde hair was held back loosely to fall around her shoulders in a profusion of curls. She wore a dress of a deep twilight-blue, with golden accents to mimic armor—and whether it was sheer stupidity or knowledge of some additional information, she did not look even faintly intimidated by him.

"Good morning," she said as pleasantly as if they had met over the breakfast table. "My name is Delia. I have a business proposition for you."

He tried to untangle this. His mind was still fogged from sleep, but it didn't escape his notice that a grimy man sleeping out in the open was hardly a good bet for a business proposition. He settled for raising one eyebrow as he stood, assumed a wary but solid stance, and folded his arms.

"Let's hear it, then."

Delia smiled again. "My employer is one of the foremost dealers of precious items in Heffog," she explained. "A client has come to us with very exacting specifications, and we have found the piece that will please them. We need you to get it for us."

"I can only assume you mean by stealing it," he said drily, "as most wealthy people do not sleep on abandoned rooftops."

She nodded.

"Why me?" he asked.

"Because one of my agents saw you climb to the roof last night," she said simply. "Add to that the fact that you are unknown in the city and appear to have no loyalty to any particular faction, and you serve our purposes quite well. You will be generously paid, of course."

Ben sighed and rubbed his forehead. "I take it this isn't a friendly offer so much as forced volunteering."

"Oh, no." She dimpled and shook her golden curls slightly. "It is an offer only. Should you refuse, no harm will come to you."

He stared suspiciously at her.

"My employer prefers to do business voluntarily," Delia said, "as they find it makes them less likely to be stabbed in their sleep."

"I, uh—" He choked and coughed. "I see. Yes."

"Perhaps you would like to hear more about the job?" the woman suggested calmly.

"I'm not sure I would." He gave her a tight smile and was about to ask her to leave when his stomach betrayed him by growling loudly.

Delia was not gauche enough to comment on that directly. She merely waited as if utterly immune to his weak half-rejection.

"I'm not sure this is a part of the city I want to get involved in," he said. He did not want to do this, but he also knew he had little choice.

In all honesty, he had almost decided to ask Prima to pull him out of this part of the game. He had mucked it up beyond repair. By now, normally, he would have tapped out and wasn't quite sure why he stuck with it this time.

Perhaps he was getting stupider as he got older.

"This part of the city?" the woman echoed.

"People fighting for petty reasons," Ben said bluntly. "There's enough cruelty already and enough terrible things being done to the powerless. I don't know why I would spend my time and effort helping one of the powerful get a bauble they want."

"Your time and effort," she said thoughtfully. She looked at him, her expression one of real interest.

"Yes!" His pride was pricked. "You know, the things that led you to seek me out. I may not be a renowned thief, but I do have skills to work with, you know, and I want to do good things for this city."

"Good things?"

"Like stop the damned slave trade, for one," he told her flatly. "So how's that for an answer? Do you think your employer would still approve of me now?"

"You want to stop the slave trade." She moved to look out over the city from the rooftop. Whoever she was, he noted she did not seem to be worried about being seen.

He wasn't foolish enough to stand beside her—he didn't want to be tipped off the roof—but he did approach and stand a few feet away from her. From there, he could see a faint glimmer of the ocean. They weren't far from it and there were only a few streets and jumbled roofs between them and the water.

"Yes," he said. "I want to stop the slave trade—and I won't be put off by people telling me that direct action won't do anything."

"Direct action?" She looked at him with a smile.

"Assassination," Ben told her.

He hoped to make her flinch but she didn't. Instead, she considered his statement.

"Assassination," she murmured. It was clear that this wasn't a prompt but rather something she thought about very carefully. At length, she nodded. "Our purposes can quite easily align, then. You see, the job would bring you within range of one of the foremost slave traders in the city."

"Really?"

Delia nodded. "They represent a not-insubstantial portion of the slave trade, which would falter following their death."

Caution made him think before he spoke.

"I'll want to confirm that myself," he said. "You understand I cannot simply take your word for it."

"Of course." She didn't look at him but she did not seem insulted in the least.

"Don't you think your employer would mind you agreeing to an assassination?" he probed.

"No." Until now, everything in her manner had invited conversation. This statement did not.

Ben looked away. "Give me a moment to think."

She nodded silently and he turned away to pace. His mind raced through his options. Without Elantria's help, he had two main choices—leave the city or try to make it on his own. If he chose to leave, he would forfeit this chance to learn the skills Prima wanted him to learn.

He looked at his hands and wiggled the fingers slightly.

What are you thinking about? Prima asked.

"Whether I should stay and take the job or leave Heffog," he told her. He was careful to keep his voice low.

The AI didn't speak for a long moment.

"I've messed everything up again," he said. "Except, not—I didn't do anything *wrong*. It's only that people are always so unreasonable. They get used to problems and they don't want someone to fix them." He folded his arms and stared out at the city. "They don't want someone to be blunt with them. Or take decisive action."

"Mmm," the AI said finally. *"So, you've been in this situation before."*

"Not this exact one." He grinned. "Assassination and high-end jewelry thievery are not my usual areas of operation. But, yeah. Like I said last night, this wouldn't be the first place I've had to leave because people didn't like my style."

"To see if I understand, you solve people's problems but they do not appreciate that?"

"Exactly." Ben nodded.

"And then, once you have taken decisive action, it becomes too uncomfortable to remain in that community?"

"Yes."

"I see." She said nothing more.

"It's infuriating," he told her. "They *say* they want the problems solved, but they only see obstacles. I solve the problem and suddenly, they're upset."

Prima held her tongue.

"Are you going to comment?" he asked her.

"I am fairly certain that my assessment would not meet with approval."

Of course. He should have expected that response. Irritated, he glowered at the sky and sighed as he looked out at the city. The AI was on everyone else's side. Of course, she would be. He was disappointed, though. She wasn't a normal person. If anyone could understand, he would think it would be her.

"Fine. Tell me what you think."

She didn't ask him if he was sure and took him at face value. He decided he liked that.

"Very well," she said. *"I will draw from the example of Elantria as I am not familiar with your other experiences. In that case, it was you who first identified slavery as a problem rather than her asking for your help regarding it. Both she and Orien cautioned you against hasty decisions that could negatively impact the very people you hoped to save, but*

you did not seek information to find out why they believed that or what the risks might be."

Ben stood rigidly but listened to each sentence carefully.

"There is a very large area of uncertainty around complex issues," Prima continued. *"It is difficult to know which course of action will be best but it seems only logical that stopping to examine the exact situation would produce better results."*

He bit his lip. "So, you're saying…"

"I am saying," Prima said with a great deal more gentleness than he had expected, *"that in my admittedly limited experience with you, I have noticed that you tend to be motivated by the sincere desire to solve problems quickly. Your morals are unwavering. The issue others have seems to stem from the fact that your desire for quick action does not allow for information-gathering and thus, your actions may do more harm than good."*

In silence, he lowered his face into his hands.

"I think, from our discussion last night, that you have already begun to mull over that same issue," she said. *"I won't tell you that Jorys was innocent or that he did not deserve justice. The question to ask yourself is simply how you can best achieve justice in a way that does not do further harm to his victims."*

She paused as if to give him time to respond, but he made no effort to do so.

"What are you thinking?"

"That I can look at my life and see a thousand things I did wrong and a thousand situations I made worse," he said bluntly.

"That is an overreaction and you know it." Her answer was immediate. *"The matter before you is how best to use your skills for the people of Heffog. Not to mention how best to heal yourself."*

"Right." Ben shook his head and looked at Delia. Whether she'd noticed his conversation or not, he wasn't sure. She smiled blandly at him. "I'll do it. But I want more information first and I want to speak to your employer."

"Done," she agreed. She gestured to the side of the building, where a ladder led to the ground.

He stepped closer to it but stopped at the edge of the roof.

The woman looked expectantly at him. "Yes?"

"You played me," he said slowly. He ran their conversation through his mind.

She frowned slightly. "I'm not familiar with that expression."

"You merely repeated what I said until I told you everything I wanted, then you offered me that."

"And you're…upset?" She looked bemused. "You get what you want, and we get what we want. Surely that's not a problem but instead, a welcome solution."

Ben sensed that it was useless to try to make her admit that she could as easily use that skill for bad purposes as good ones. He shrugged and followed her but told himself he would have to keep his guard up. It was all well and good to pretend that people could find mutually agreeable solutions most of the time.

But you only found out who people *really* were when the two of you couldn't agree.

CHAPTER TWENTY

Unlike Elantria, Delia did not travel on foot through the city. A carriage waited when she and Ben reached the street and she held the door open for him before she followed him into the shadowed interior. Black gauze hung over the windows to obscure their features from curious passers-by, and the carriage had no coat of arms.

He replayed what Prima had said in his mind.

It was difficult to keep his thoughts from circling to the single, horrifying memory of the slaves stumbling out of Jorys' study. They were terrified and powerless. That fear haunted him.

Every moment he spent dwelling on it was a moment he didn't spend trying to fix it.

With Prima's blunt words in his head, he could see now that the merchant had merely been one point in a web. The people in that room hadn't been frightened because he sold them but because so many others would collaborate with him to keep them enslaved. The guards would prevent them from escaping while they were brought to the market, the authorities wouldn't intervene when they were sold, and the people wouldn't rise up and stand in the way of them being sent off to God only knew where.

What he needed to do was to bring the entire network down. Not only that, he needed to salt the ground so thoroughly that nothing would ever grow in its place.

But that wasn't possible. At least, no solution came to him. He could hear all the mealy-mouthed advice now—people telling him to provide profitable industries for the slave traders to switch to. But why should the city be rewarded with new industry when it had profited for so long off the fear and enslavement of others?

He had no clue what to do and he was damned certain that Elantria's approach wasn't doing any better than his. His hands clenched, and when he looked up, he saw Delia watching him.

She didn't say anything and simply leaned back in her seat and stared out the window as the city rolled past. They were heading east to the district where the richest of the rich lived, and he took the time to consider what this said about her employer. A rich person who wanted to prey on the other rich? Who collaborated to steal the prized possessions of fellow nobles? It didn't add up.

When he arrived, he realized why it didn't add up. It wasn't a noble doing this.

It was a servant.

The carriage brought them to a small gate at the back of a walled compound, where they stepped out in a small courtyard. It was humble but swept clean. Against the outer wall stood a two-story house, grand by the standards of the city but dwarfed by the mansion that lay at the center of the compound.

Delia, who now wore a dull cloak over her dress, brought him inside. A man with blue-green hair and black eyes looked up from a table where he studied a building layout. He rolled it carefully before he approached quickly and held a hand out.

"I am Nemon," he said and seemed unperturbed by his visitor's searching gaze. "I am the product of many generations of by-blows," he said with little emotion. "The nobles mingle more with their servants than they would have you believe."

Ben swallowed, unsure what to say to this. "I'm Ben," he said. On a whim, he added, "Nothing about my lineage is noteworthy."

It seemed his instinct had been correct because the man responded with a genuine grin. "As you can see from my residence, lineage is more about the circumstance of birth than about the parentage of an individual."

He looked around. "That's true in comparison to the main house. And yet, you have your house in this compound. That suggests a certain favor."

"Well." Nemon returned to the table. "My…owners…were not certain whether to place their trust in the new elven king and thus, only half the household has departed to maintain a residence in the new capital with the lady of the house. The husband remains and the rest of us have more space than usual. Certain complications have arisen in my business since the shift but also certain opportunities."

"Why do you do it?" he asked him simply. "Delia says you steal from the nobles and give to other nobles. Why take such a risk?"

The man propped himself on the edge of the table as he considered this. One leg swung slowly. "Because I can," he said simply. "Unlike the vast majority of this city, I have no reverence for my relatives. I understand that their blood is no different from mine and I have grown up among them, so their mannerisms are not a mystery to me. They give or deny birthright on capricious grounds, so I take whatever I can lay my hands on. What is it to me which noble has a particular necklace if I get a good fee for supplying it?" He shrugged.

Ben looked at him in silence. Nemon was one of the people who had found his place in the current system, a peripheral member of the web. Whether from apathy or greed, he was not interested in tearing the system down. He would simply grift from it.

He did not even pretend that he had selfless motives for doing so.

"Perhaps you'll feel differently when Delia tells you what I demanded as my price," he said.

"Oh?" The man focused on Delia.

"He wants to assassinate the mark while he's there," she said flatly. She smiled when her employer laughed.

"You...don't mind?" Ben asked, a little unnerved.

"Not in the slightest," Nemon said. "After all, the confusion after a noble is killed is ripe ground for theft—as are the auction and transfer of goods that follow."

Now, he felt a growing unease. The slave traders of Heffog were not people he felt charitably toward, but he also felt that the act of killing deserved gravity. The man was apparently willing to view life and death as matters that affected his business and nothing more.

It was unnerving to find that he preferred Elantria's inaction to this cheerful self-interest. He wondered what she would say to this and wished he could ask her.

No. That door is closed.

"So, what's your plan?" Nemon continued to swing his leg and seemed genuinely interested.

"I'm not sure yet," he replied and pointed at the table. "Is that the layout of the house in question?"

"Yes." The other two exchanged a glance and Delia gave a small nod. Having been assured that the recruit was trustworthy, the man went to the table and unrolled the map. "The necklace is here in the family's personal vault. It's an ancient piece, very valuable but not well-known these days. It should be quite a long time before anyone notices that it's missing."

"So why does your client want it?" he questioned.

"I don't ask those things," Nemon told him. "It's one of my guarantees. In any event, the necklace looks like..." He pulled a sketched rendering from a pile "This."

Ben studied it. He wasn't an expert on jewelry, but he had to admit that he found it more gaudy than anything else. To him, it looked like nothing more than a wild jumble of large stones and pearls crusted over a thick piece of metal in no particular pattern.

"Are you sure they don't merely want it for the jewels?" he asked dubiously.

"Again, I do not ask." The man smiled. "Exactly as I will not ask *your* reasons for wishing to assassinate the owner."

He grew less comfortable by the minute.

"Tell me about the owner," he said.

"You've signed on, then?"

"Yes." He didn't allow himself time to hesitate. If he did, he knew he'd leave and make new enemies—powerful ones who didn't mind killing.

If he stayed, he gained access to someone who could help him destroy the nobility one by one, at least until the man realized he was ending the gravy train. And, hell, if he stole enough items for him, Nemon might not even mind.

Sometimes, to do good, you had to resort to unpleasant means. He reminded himself of what had happened at the fae castle.

"Very good." His new employer gestured to a seating area around the fireplace. The furniture was worn and the expensive fabric faded and threadbare. "Come, sit. We will talk." He waved for Delia to join them.

"Don't you cause suspicion by coming here?" Ben asked her curiously.

"Oh, no." She leaned back in her chair. "I'm known around the city as a courtesan. I often arrive at various estates in insufficient disguises, usually at back gates."

"A courtesan?" He had to admit a courtesan would make a good ally for a thief.

"I said I'm *known* as a courtesan," she corrected.

"Ah."

"It means no one tries to marry me and I get to go almost anywhere I want." Her dimples returned. "It's perfect."

Ben could only smile. There was something amusing about her taking joy from what others probably tried to shame her for.

"She's not mentioning," Nemon said, "that she runs a boarding house for runaway courtesans and sets them up with new identities in new cities."

"I don't make fun of how *you* spend *your* money," Delia protested.

He looked from one to the other. It was interesting to see the range of morality various people in this city had. And if Delia worked with Nemon, the half-elf couldn't be all that bad, surely.

"Who's the mark?" he asked.

"Lord Kerill," Nemon stated.

"Who's his heir?"

The man looked curious. "His niece, Birra."

A thought had begun to take shape in his head. Elantria had said that one of the problems with his assassination of Jorys was that the slave trade would only accelerate under any of his heirs. If he wanted to not make the same mistake again, he had to be careful.

"What's her opinion of his business?" he asked.

"She already runs some of it."

Ah. Not an ally, then.

"And what if she's dead?" he asked. "Or otherwise unable to claim the inheritance."

"She'd better be dead," Nemon warned him. "If she's not, she'll fight tooth and nail. Behind her in line, you see, is his son—who's quite the abolitionist."

Ben allowed himself a satisfied smile. Excellent. "And how difficult would it be to forge a letter with Kerill's seal?" he asked.

His employer now looked deeply interested. "Not overly. It can be done if you need it. For a price, of course. What would you like it to say?"

"That he has repented of his dealings after a religious experience and intends to make his son his heir. Oh, and he will have the son help him unravel his business and put the fortune to work fighting the slavery industry in Heffog."

"You plan to pin his murder on Birra," Delia said quietly.

"Yes. Yes, I do." His smile was grim.

"That's...sneaky." Prima sounded almost worried. *"And—what's the human term? 'Ice cold?'"*

He gave a tiny nod to tell her she was correct. "Do you think it will work?" he asked Nemon.

"Oh, very well." The man was deeply amused. "And would I be correct that you will kill Birra as well to make sure?"

"Of course."

"You will make an interesting addition to the city." Nemon studied him. "Already, you've been seen in the company of Kural and Elantria and now, I find you're an assassin." He tapped his mouth and raised an eyebrow. "Did she hire you to kill Jorys?"

"No," Ben said and added nothing further. He didn't want to talk about Elantria, nor did he want to make it seem like she had anything to do with the merchant's death.

"A mystery!" The man seemed delighted by that. "Very well, keep your secrets. I'll find a time in the near future when Birra will be at Kerill's house and we'll get you in to accomplish both goals."

CHAPTER TWENTY-ONE

When Jacob arrived at the lab in the morning, a box rested on one of the tables with several staff members gathered around it.

"What's that?"

"It's for you," Amber said. She waved a hand at it.

"It's…okay, we've checked that it's not a bomb, right?" The hate mail had mostly tapered off after the initial burst of publicity, but some people were still not happy about the idea of virtual reality.

"It's not a bomb," she said and rolled her eyes good-naturedly. "Nick brought it."

"Oh. Okay, then." He put his cup of coffee down and stepped closer to open the box. The cake inside was his favorite kind—funfetti with boring white frosting. As Amber said, it was the "basic bitch" of cakes.

He had argued that one should not tamper with perfection.

CONGRATULATIONS was written across the top in blue frosting.

"Congratulations?" he asked.

"Yes." Amber reached under the table and pulled out a bottle of champagne. "Taigan and Jamie were able to see each other in-game for a while."

"Holy shit!"

After the disappointing first meeting, everyone in the team had been in a funk. The girl's undeniable progress toward consciousness constantly encountered snags they hadn't realized there could be, and he had doubted that they could truly help her. But this brought hope.

He smiled at the group. "Holy shit," he repeated. "Gimme that champagne." He popped the cork to the sound of cheers and put his mouth hastily over the opening when contents began to fountain out.

"Okay, that's *his* bottle," Amber said to the others. She retrieved another one.

The cake was cut and served—breakfast for the team coming in and dessert for the team heading home. Everyone watched the video of Taigan and Jamie fighting the jackalopes, and raucous laughter erupted as both teenagers went full berserker in their individual special ways.

"It's working," Jacob said to Nick and Amber in an undertone. "I can't believe it. I had...stopped believing it."

"Me too," she admitted.

"Yeah, me too." Nick sighed. "I felt like such a shitbag, too, having spoken to them all and...like you said, we shouldn't get too invested, but I did. I thought it would be easy—and it's very definitely not."

"Not in the least," she agreed. "And we should have thought of that tactic sooner, you know—mortal danger and all that. It was one of the key pieces DuBois talked about at the start."

"Yeah, how stupid of us," he quipped. "Going easy on the comatose girl."

"Okay, point taken. Still." Amber finished her last mouthful of cake with a happy sigh. "Finally, a good update for her parents. Plus, she said she wants to see them all."

"And there's no way that forcing them all into mortal danger together could backfire on us," Jacob said mildly.

Nick chortled and reached for another piece of cake.

"I don't suppose Ben has also had any leaps forward while I was gone?" the other man asked hopefully.

"Greedy," Amber admonished. "Isn't one piece of good news enough for you? But since you ask, he continues to gain his coordination at a frankly astonishing rate. Last night, he climbed a building on his own. Although that was after he assassinated someone and was kicked out by the person sheltering him."

Jacob put his fork down. "I'm sorry, he *what?*"

His partners exchanged a look. They tested their wills against each other for a moment and, when neither backed down, sighed and played a round of rock-paper-scissors. She lost and recounted the story of what had happened.

"Fuck, I might have done the same," Jacob admitted. "I didn't even know there was slavery in this world."

"There's a lot we didn't get to discover because the game wasn't developed," she pointed out. "We simply input all the lore and let the procedural generator guide people through it. Our players are seeing parts of the game that we've never seen."

"Mmm, maybe we want more QA on our end before we roll new zones out to players."

"Quite possibly." Amber tapped her foot. "Ugh. I'm supposed to sleep but I drank way too much coffee for that."

"I'll go home," Nick suggested.

"You do it, you die."

"I merely offered." He stood and served himself a third piece of cake. "Anyway, Jacob, about Ben… His doctors keep calling to ask if our progress metrics are correct. They insist that he shouldn't be able to do any of the things he did when we took him out last time, much less what he can do in the game."

"Well, they can argue about it all they want." The other man took a long sip of coffee. "He's on video doing all of it, so it's indisputable."

"I think they're more worried that they didn't think of using this system." Nick shrugged. "Or, it might be that they don't like it because they can't understand why it works. DuBois says that's it, but it doesn't make sense to me."

"As a doctor, I am telling you that a lack of clarity is *precisely* why they dispute it." DuBois approached, holding his customary bag of popcorn. "There is any number of vital, useful, effective treatments that have never been utilized because doctors could not find the underlying mechanism and didn't want to prescribe it."

"Just when you thought you knew all the things to be angry about," Nick muttered to the others.

"Well, while you spend time being angry about it, I may have a solution." The doctor took a seat on one of the lab stools. "I've been in contact with some neuroscientists who study proprioception and kinesthesia to ask if avatar control in virtual reality might not be subject to the same constraints as moving a body."

As per usual, it took the others a moment to parse his words.

"Wait," Jacob said.

"Because he thinks of himself as someone who can control his body," Amber said slowly, "he's more able to bring his virtual self into line with that?"

"Exactly." DuBois nodded at her. "Much like the fact that Justin and Dotty were able to use magic—or that Taigan can summon objects." Somewhat testily, he added, "*That* should not be possible."

"Now, now, simply because you can't explain it..." Nick gave him a bland smile and quailed when he glared at him. "It's a joke, a play on your words earlier."

Jacob ignored them. "So because his actual physiology doesn't get in the way quite as much, it means he was able to re-learn the movement pathways more easily in the pod and it continues when he wakes up? Do I have that right?"

DuBois nodded.

"Huh." Jacob chewed as he thought and helped himself to another piece of cake. He hadn't bought breakfast on the way there, so the cake was welcome. "Does *he* know how well he's doing, statistically speaking?"

Amber shook her head. "I don't think so. Eliza told him that he's doing off-the-charts well, but I don't think he fully absorbed that."

"He was distracted," Jacob observed. "What with his crush and all."

"They're so cute together." She grinned.

"In the *meantime*," DuBois said, clearly hoping to hasten the conversation along from this topic, "as Jacob has astutely pointed out, self-doubt could be fatal. Ben appears to not know how unusual his abilities are, and I say we continue to challenge him—not so much that he gives up but enough that he doesn't stop to dwell on how far he's come."

"We should be able to arrange that," she said dryly. "Now that he's gone all hitman on us. Boy, was that a turnaround."

"It has been strange to watch," the doctor conceded.

"Very John Wick-ish," Nick agreed. "But on the other hand, he is stepping out on his own and that's good."

"True." Amber scrunched her face and leaned on the table. "Okay, maybe another piece of cake…" She reached for the server before her conscience could intrude.

"Personalities can appear to change wildly when push comes to shove," Jacob said. "And we've seen this in other patients. It's not only him. Justin had much more of a background in video games so the killing didn't faze him like it did with Ben and Dotty, but even *he* came out of it wanting to make a difference in the world."

"Yes," she said and grimaced, "but if Ben comes out of this as a hitman, we can expect some uncomfortable questions."

"Maybe he's merely doing what *you* suggested and exploring his morality in a world without the same constraints and permanence as this one," Jacob countered. "Remember that?"

"Oh, right." Amber hunched her shoulders. "I hope that's what it is, anyway. I don't want to embroil us in endless lawsuits when a vigilante hops through various countries assassinating dictators."

"Don't worry," he told her. "The best-case scenario is that, at this rate, he'll have swung to full-on pacifist again in a few days. If not...we sell this to the military as an assassin training program."

She punched him in the shoulder and laughed. "Stop it. Okay, I'll try to sleep. If anything cool happens, get more cake."

"There's half left," Nick protested.

"And you cretins will be around it for eight hours. I don't think there'll be any left when I get back." She smiled at them and wandered off to retrieve her coat.

Jacob smiled after her.

"How's it going with you two?" Nick asked him.

"It's going fine." He glared warningly. The manipulation might have worked out well in some ways, but he wasn't entirely ready to let his friend off the hook.

Not to mention that both he and Amber were a great deal more cautious in relationships than they had been at eighteen when the world seemed like a giant game with no consequences. They had skirted a few issues for a week now, including who got keys to whose home and whether there would be any PDA in the lab. Neither of them was yet willing to talk about the issues.

It was the kind of minefield of a conversation that would make everything much easier but was utterly terrifying to have for no good reason.

From the look on Nick's face, he knew some of what was

going on. Thankfully, before he could say anything about it, DuBois broke the tension by crinkling the cellophane on his popcorn bag loudly.

"Damn," he said. "I'm already out."

"You could mix it up with some cake," Nick suggested.

"No, thank you." The doctor drifted away to the breakroom, where his popcorn inhabited almost half the cupboards.

"How that man is not malnourished is beyond me," Jacob said.

His friend nodded gravely. "I think he's a robot."

CHAPTER TWENTY-TWO

Lord Kerill's ancestors had been some of the first elven nobles to take up residence in Heffog. When they arrived, the settlement was nothing more than a few huts with human fishermen and an area on a nearby cliff where the caravans could camp while selling goods or buying them.

The Kerills had bought almost all the land. With a combination of cunning and outright lies, they had bought the houses in which the fishermen lived, the piers at which the boats docked, and the camping grounds where the caravans stayed.

Not everything that happened after that was bad. Trade flourished in Heffog, a link between Insea and the countries it could not reach easily by land. The family had connections to any goods people wanted to sell and the more trade flourished, the more new buildings were bought. Land nearby was tilled for crops, silver was discovered in the hills and mined, and a trade sprang up in medicines and ointments made from the bounty of the sea.

Increasingly, elven nobles came to make their home in the city. There was nowhere to fall in Insea and nothing to be lost—but nothing to play for, either. By contrast, Heffog always seemed to be on the verge of something. It never became the center of any trade route, yet it was a hub on many and indispensable. As it became richer, so did the nobles who owned it.

When the new elven monarchy was established to challenge Insea, many families left outright and sold their land to Kerill or to the merchants who wanted to rise in the world. On the one hand, it was a coup, a chance to snatch up the land that had slipped from the family's grasp over the years.

On the other, it was the sign of change, and change could doom old money.

Lord Kerill had not been one to sit by and watch his family's fortunes diminish. Slavery had been rare in Heffog before the elven nobles left and there was a strong prohibition against it in elven culture. Other races must be subjugated via trade and armies, or so the wisdom went. If one could not prove one's superiority via cunning or military might, one was *not* superior.

The present incumbent did not particularly care about that. Slavery was profitable and that was enough for him. The dearth of elven nobles meant that fewer disagreed with him on the matter, and he took that as a license to continue.

It was what had caused the rift between him and his son, however. Once close, the two men had diverged sharply on this issue. His son now sought—both legally and less legally—to undo everything his father did, while Kerill—unexpectedly, in Ben's opinion—did everything in his power to bring his son into the fold again.

That was the twist that made his plan better than he had even imagined. Birra had worked hard to make herself a worthy successor, but everyone knew there was a chance that Kerill would make peace with his son. A notably ruthless woman, she might do anything if she thought her hard-earned inheritance would be lost.

Nemon, who knew a great deal about the family—he decided to not ask how—forged the letter himself. It had the understated, self-important tone of elven nobles yet still held the pathos of a parent begging a child to return. It announced Kerill's intention to cease his operations and do anything his son wished to restore their relationship.

Birra would be furious. He considered letting her find the letter and murder Kerill herself, but there was too much of a chance that her father would deny it and their hand would be tipped.

He snuck into the house at dawn when the courtyard at the back of the manor was bustling. Farmers on their way into Heffog would stop first at the wealthy houses to give cooks the first choice of vegetables and fruits from the country. Carts with bolts of cloth, herbs, or animals also called there to trade.

In the crush of people and shouting, it was fairly easy for him to gain entry without raising suspicion. As a cart unloaded burlap sacks of grain, he hefted one over his shoulder and strode into the house—after staggering sideways, of course. Not only was his coordination not what it should be, he hadn't ever carried a huge sack of grain before.

While he was an unknown, no one thought to stop him because he brought the grain into the house. His expression carefully neutral, he followed another porter to a basement and piled his bag of grain next to theirs. He dawdled so the man ascended the stairs ahead of him. Once he was alone, he slipped quickly into the shadows to explore the storerooms.

As he had expected, there were other routes into the house—and, to his relief, many places to hide.

With surprising patience, Ben waited. His supply of food was easily accessible—and better than he would have outside—and he had various locations where he could remain undiscovered. He waited for almost two days while he mapped the quiet times for the house and the voices of those who came and went. To occupy himself, he practiced moving his fingers by sorting beans and counting grains of rice. He drew and redrew the floor plan of the dwelling in the hard-packed dirt of the floor and removed all trace of it each time.

In the deep of the night before the second dawn, he made his move.

He had studied people as they ascended and descended the stairs so now knew which creaked and which did not. Also, he knew where the guards patrolled. He snuck up a set of stairs that ended somewhere along the side of the house and listened at the doorway.

The silence was encouraging.

As quietly as he could, he unlatched the door and began to open it. There was no movement beyond, although there was some light.

Ben looked out into a small antechamber off the kitchen. This room held large bowls, a wooden barrel of flour, and jars of spices, along with a heavy wooden table for kneading bread and making pastries.

Better still, it was uninhabited at this time of night. He slipped into the room and closed the door almost entirely. It made sense to leave an easily accessible escape route.

The vault that held Kerill's jewels was part of his study. The room contained a false wall that could be activated by pressing one of the carved fish on the wooden panels behind the desk.

What the elf seemed to *not* know was that there was another entrance to it. A very different mechanism was concealed in the library, a sliding panel behind one of the bookshelves. "Like many old houses," Nemon had said with a smile, "there were more secrets built into it than have been remembered."

He now needed to find that library, although he knew where it was, of course—he had mapped the house out in paces while he was in the basement. His target destination was about twenty yards to his left but he had no idea what occupants he might find in the corridors between here and there.

The first step, though, was to get through the kitchen. He

paused at the open doorway, listened intently, and counted two different snores plus breathing from others, although he couldn't tell how many.

There was nothing for it. He would have to look. Caution made him pause to confirm that he wouldn't cast a shadow when he poked his head out before he stepped slightly around the door.

The kitchens were massive. The light came from banked fires in three hearths. Ropes of garlic and onions hung from the ceiling, along with sausages, haunches of meat, and—in his opinion—far too much fish. One of the cooks dozed in a big chair by the fire, while another slept on a bench nearby. How they didn't fall off, he wasn't sure, but they seemed to have considerable practice.

The quiet breathing came from a young woman who stared at the fire. She looked dwarven to his eyes, although she might simply have been a very short human, and she did something that looked very much like amateur magic. It wasn't the kind Zaara did but rather what he was familiar with from his world—a scattering of leaves and a diagram on the floor.

Hopefully, she would remain engrossed in it while he snuck out. He considered how best to creep across the tiles. There was no path that would take him from his current position to the door without her seeing him…unless he crawled.

Well, there was no point in clinging to his dignity. Ben grimaced, lowered himself to all fours, and crawled painstakingly across the floor. He went under a table that had drips of blood under it, silently bemoaned the fact that there was no such thing as hand sanitizer there, and stopped near the door to listen for guards.

No one seemed to be patrolling the corridor.

He snuck out of the kitchen and into the hallway.

It was quiet, which was a boon. On the first night, there had been a big dinner of some kind and guards had patrolled for an hour or so after everyone left. Tonight, there had been nothing of the sort.

He was surprised to see a light still burning in the study and heard the murmur of voices. Was Kerill still up and working? That gave him a moment's grudging respect for the man. Unfortunately, it also meant he had to be quieter in the vault.

The door to the library was locked but the mechanism was old. He was able to pick it with only two of the tools and eased inside. A magical lantern kept the room illuminated in a reddish hue of light he assumed was to preserve the books but which made the space look like a horror-movie set.

Ben found the panel and opened it. It wasn't complicated, but there was a difference between "simple" and "easy." For one thing, it hadn't been opened in generations and would almost certainly creak. He lifted it an inch and took another tool from his belt, a long piece of wire with an oil-soaked cloth around it. Working quickly, he wiped the cloth up and around all the mechanisms he could find and repeated the process every inch until the panel was open and he could release it.

By then, his entire body ached, he had a crick in his neck, and he didn't care overly much about the damned necklace.

Still, he was in place now. He retrieved his next tool, a small crystal infused with magic and encased in a metal pyramid. When he flipped one of the sides open, a dim light illuminated everything around him.

The first thing he discovered was that elven nobles preserved the jawbones of their ancestors. It was a revelation that made him jerk back, fling the pyramid in the air—he wasn't quite sure why—and curl into a ball on the ground. He barely managed to uncurl in time to catch the artifact before it clanged noisily and alerted Kerill, and he sat for a moment, glowering at the bones.

Honestly, who hid *bones* in a vault? Ashes in an urn, he could understand. In a mausoleum or somewhere you wouldn't stumble on physical skeletons by accident.

Of course, he *was* robbing the guy.

Ben gave himself a moment to gather his focus before he pushed to his feet and began his search. He looked over his shoulder every few seconds as if to make sure the jawbones hadn't come down from the wall to attack him.

Involuntarily, he shuddered.

The necklace was where Nemon had said it would be—in a jewelry box that took a great deal of finagling before he could open it silently. Not only that, but it also took several attempts to make each movement work. He was better at fine motor control but he was far from perfect at it.

He had barely slipped the necklace—it was as ugly in person as he'd thought—into a pouch at his waist when a commotion sounded from the back of the house. In a panic, he pulled the door closed behind him and stood frozen in the darkness.

How did they know he was there? No one had seen him. He was sure of that.

Unless there were spells in the room that triggered some kind of alarm. He waited, his eyes closed in terror as booted footsteps drew closer to the library...and passed it. The door to the study slammed open.

"What is the meaning of this?" Lord Kerill demanded.

"My lord, apologies for the late hour." The guard sounded respectful. "But we captured the elf you said would try to break into the property."

Ben's eyebrows raised. He crept carefully toward the second door that led to the study. There was a faint gap where lamplight shone through but not enough to see anything. *Dammit.*

Orders were issued and a scuffling sound followed.

"So." Lord Kerill spoke coldly. "Orien Markes. It's been quite some time since I've seen you."

Orien? He froze in shock.

The elf said nothing, however.

"And why are you here? Is it to kill me like you killed the

merchant Jorys? It seems your beloved Elantria is not the pacifist you thought she was."

"I'm not here to kill you," Orien said tightly.

"I'm afraid I can't simply take your word for that." Kerill sounded amused now. "You understand, I'm sure. Unfortunately, it means I will have to execute you. There's no other option, you see."

Shit. Ben froze, his hand on the panel. The room was full of guards and he had barely a hope in hell of escaping before he and Orien died, but he couldn't simply leave the other man there. After all, he was the reason the elf was in trouble now.

Before he could give himself time to chicken out, he pushed the door open and tackled the first person he saw.

CHAPTER TWENTY-THREE

Whether fortunately or unfortunately was debatable, the first person Ben saw could only be Lord Kerill's niece. She was tall, with an angular face and pale blue eyes that seemed to glow in a darker blue face. Blue-black hair was held back in an ornate braid and she wore a gown crusted with silver embroidery and jewels. It honestly *hurt* to land on it. While he had never considered the idea that he might get a puncture wound from a sapphire, it seemed very likely.

He stared at her in shock and she returned it with an outraged glare.

"Who the *hell* are you?" she demanded. "What *human* was allowed into the family vault? I'll see you punished for this."

The threat confirmed that she was indeed the niece. He pushed to his feet and looked around to run a hasty headcount.

Lord Kerill, Birra—still on the floor—Orien, held by his injured arm and who stared at him in genuine shock, and two guards in the room and probably more at the door.

His first thought was that he could kill the slave trader and maybe he should. The man was a monster. He objected even to Elantria's methods and he was willing to kill Orien rather than have him jailed. His family had owned the city for generations and, rather than rest on the hoard of wealth he had already accumulated, he resorted to slave trading.

Logic and justice demanded that he should kill him. The city would be better off.

But he had only a split second, a single chance to save Orien. He cast a single, pained look at Kerill, marked the lines on the man's face, and thought of the forged letter in the pouch at his hip.

With immense regret, he gave up on the perfect plan.

He charged the guard who held Orien's arm before anyone could try to apprehend him. Perhaps the man hadn't viewed him as an armed threat because he hadn't come out with weapons. He had no time to realize how wrong he was before the knife sank into his neck. With a gurgle, he sank to his knees and blood spurted from the wound.

"Gah! Fuck!" Ben swiped at the blood on his face.

Orien's shock dissolved at his words. He whipped around and looped his chains around the other guard's neck. With a well-practiced motion, he spun the man and used the chains to break his neck before he jerked them free.

"Come on!" the elf snapped.

"Right." He brandished the bloody knife at Kerill and Birra, both frozen in horror, as he backed toward the door.

She recovered first. "Guards!"

"Fuck," Orien said succinctly. He unlatched the door and leapt aside, pushing his companion with him so the guards streamed past them and into the room. As soon as the last man cleared the doorway, he caught Ben's shirt and yanked him into the corridor. "Run," the elf said.

He didn't need to be told twice. The guards yelled and one had turned to follow them. He ran while the necklace bounced at his waist and he held a bloody knife in his hand. Orien clutched the chains to stop them from rattling too much and ran with grim determination.

They barreled through the kitchens and into the courtyard, but Kerill's magic caught up with them.

He wasn't a mage himself, but his family had employed the best of the best for decades. An alarm had triggered and magical red lanterns pulsed everywhere while Kerill snapped, "Intruders heading to the back gate. *Catch them.*"

Guards raced out of towers and down the road that led around the mansion.

"Fuck, fuck, fuck," Ben muttered. He looked around in panic. They should never have stopped running, he thought in despair. Five men sprinted from the walls, two more emerged from the mansion, and a few came along the road from the other direction with what sounded like a full dozen hot on their heels.

"It's not so bad," Orien said. He turned and his gaze darted quickly to assess the enemy.

"What makes you say that?" He gave him a quick look. They had ten seconds at most until the first of the guards reached them, and how could they possibly fight this many?

"Well, if you hadn't intervened, I would already be dead. There is presently a chance that I might escape." The elf sounded almost cheerful.

"So it's only better for *you*," he muttered. "*Great.*" He had a short-sword and nothing else, and all his muscles were shaking.

"Now, now." Orien was—infuriatingly—grinning.

"Did you have any follow up to that?"

"Not really. I was about to point out that you voluntarily intervened to help me, but that seemed in poor taste." He flashed a smile. "Ah, I think I know what to do. Head to the left corner of that house there, on my mark."

"And then what?"

"Then we'll see, won't we?"

"I swear to God," he muttered, "if I had a better plan..."

Orien ignored his muttering. "On three. One…two…three!" He sprinted to the building he had mentioned and Ben followed.

Their unexpected departure left three sets of guards focused on a now non-existent target. Unable to stop, they careened helplessly into a mass collision. A scream indicated that at least one had met the wrong end of another's weapon.

"Keep running!" the elf said before he turned and flung his chains behind him. Another man screamed along with a noise that sounded very much like metal meeting flesh and bone.

Ben winced, tried not to hurl his dinner, and raced on.

He skidded into the shadows and turned to see the layout of the battle. Two of the guards tried to help the one who had been injured and the rest fanned out around Orien. The man he had already struck with his chains sprawled nearby and blood streamed down his face.

Hastily, Ben scanned his surroundings. He could now see why the elf had brought them this way. Behind this house was a stairway to the walls as the house itself was part of the structure. They could get out there if they could ascend the stairs and jump before the guards caught them.

And, of course, if they didn't die when they jumped. Or before that.

One of the men darted toward Orien and was kept out of range with a flick of the chains. The next time he darted in, however, another came from the other direction. Ben yelled a warning that was unnecessary as the elf's foot lashed out to catch the second attacker full in the face.

The elf was doing well so far, but there was no way he could defeat all of them.

His mind conjured an impossible thought and he heaved a sigh. There *was* a way to get out of this without much more fuss. Probably.

On the downside, he would learn what happened when Nemon was upset with someone.

"Gentlemen." He raised his voice so it carried. "You have a choice. You can choose to apprehend this one runaway slave—an unskilled laborer and useful at best as a pretty face in a nobleman's house." He avoided meeting Orien's curious gaze and drew the necklace out. "Or you can retrieve your lord's heirloom. If you waste time apprehending the slave, I'll be long gone with something a hundred times as valuable."

It was enough to make them stop and look at each other.

"Come on," Ben muttered. He caught his companion by the arm and shoved him toward the stairs. "Go, go, go before they start thinking!"

"Where did you *get* that?" Orien whispered in horror.

"In the vault—you know, where you saw me tumble out of. *Move!*" He tripped on the stairs and swore. The guards were running now.

He might be able to get away with the necklace but he didn't like his odds. With a sinking feeling in the pit of his stomach, he turned and threw it like a frisbee. It sailed over the guards' heads and they stopped to watch it.

Orien grasped his arm and hauled him over the edge of the wall.

"Fu—" His expletive was lost in a gurgle when he plunged into a deep pool of water.

Kerill had a moat. Of course he did.

Ben came up spluttering, flailed awkwardly to the shore and climbed out. He extended a hand to pull Orien out as well. "Come on," he muttered, panting. "We have to run."

"You think?" the elf asked acerbically. He shook his hair out of his eyes, looped the chain over his shoulders, and hurried away.

With one last look at the walls and the mansion beyond, he followed.

CHAPTER TWENTY-FOUR

They were a few streets away before Orien spoke. He darted between alleys with complete concentration, kept him back, or ushered him forward with gestures, but no words were exchanged.

When he relaxed fractionally, Ben assumed they were in Elantria's territory again. Still, he waited for his companion to break the silence first. He had made the somewhat debatable mistake of not listening to him once and he chose to use caution this time.

"So how did you wind up there?" the elf asked finally.

By his actions, he had already pissed Nemon off. He debated how much more to piss him off and decided to keep things secret for the time being. "Someone hired me to steal that necklace."

"And you wanted an opportunity at another slave trader," Orien said neutrally.

"This time was different."

"You *weren't* planning to kill him?" The elf raised an eyebrow.

"No, I was, but I intended to make sure the right person took over the family business." He frowned at his companion's skeptical expression. "I listened to what Elantria said, you know. And you."

"Not the first time."

He wanted to yell a response but he managed to bite his tongue. "No," he said through gritted teeth. "Not the first time."

Orien studied him with genuine interest. "You've changed in the past few days. What happened?" His gaze roamed impersonally over his body. "It doesn't look like you had the stuffing knocked out of you or anything."

"If you must know, I had an unflattering portrait of myself, painted by a—" He remembered how Prima had reacted to being called a demon. "A magical spirit," he finished.

"Ah." The elf looked as if he had more questions and wasn't sure which one to ask first.

They walked in silence for another block before Ben said, "I didn't want you to die or take the fall for me."

"You don't have to justify leaping to my aid, you know. That one, I appreciated." Orien sounded amused. He swung his arms slightly, still trapped by the chains.

"You don't seem at all bothered by those," he observed. "And you fight well with them."

"I was a slave a while back," the elf said. He didn't look even remotely bothered by the memory and simply shrugged. "That was when slave trading had only started to take off in Heffog. They noticed I was light on my feet so they were training me to be a gladiator. It worked out well for me. Not so well for them, though."

Ben made a mental note to not piss him off ever again.

Then something else occurred to him. "How did Kerill know you?"

"He owned me," Orien said promptly. "He took over a few of the mansions when people left for the new monarchy and I was one of the servants there. Of course, he sold most of us. He'd had a taste of how profitable it could be and there we all were. Some of us, he kept because he wanted to train us first so he could get a better price. He liked to single me out and talk to me, to remind the other slaves that elves were better. It made him look like an ass, though—if he thought elves were in any way better, why did he own me?" He shrugged. "Anyway, I killed the overseer and left with some of the others. Kerill sends messages from time to time, telling me to come back."

"Why on earth would you go back?" he demanded.

"Mmm—allegedly so he can treat me with the respect I deserve and we can both profit. Somehow, I doubt that." Orien grinned.

"So when you said I might make things worse by killing slave traders…"

"I was speaking from experience, yes. I've made it something of a hobby to examine the trade." The elf stopped and fixed him with a firm look. "I know you think Elantria is a coward. Hell, sometimes even I disagree with her methods. I wish she would take more of a stand. Then again, I was only a servant and she was an acknowledged bastard. We had different lives."

"Yeah," Ben said, "and maybe that blinds her to—"

His companion cut him off. "But she gave up much to stay here and fight for people instead of living a cushy life. So maybe…consider that before you call her a coward again."

"I don't think we'll speak again," he pointed out.

"Where did you think we were going?" Orien demanded. "Good gods, man. I'm taking you back to her."

Ben waved his hands in protest. "And you didn't think that was a bad plan? She hates me! And…the feeling is mostly mutual."

"She doesn't hate you," the elf said. "Elantria reserves hate for a very select group of people and you had better hope you never number among them. Most of them are dead and she's still trying to find ways to ruin their legacies."

"You…" He sighed. "Look, I appreciate you helping me get out. I do. But I don't think going back to Elantria is the answer."

"Well, you've pissed off the person you were supposed to get the necklace for," Orien pointed out. "And you have no other benefactors. So unless you want to bite it, I suggest you come with me." He saw the look on his face and sighed. "Okay, I'll… smooth the way. If nothing else, you earned yourself points by saving me."

Ben sighed, but he had a point. Nemon seemed like he could be a very unpleasant person if crossed and he had failed him—and in a way that would make it difficult for anyone to steal the same necklace again.

He followed the elf through the dark streets to Elantria's house after only one more caution.

"The person who hired me—he knows I was here before."

"And?" Orien looked at him.

"I don't want to bring anything down on her. If nothing else, it'll hardly help her impression of me."

"She already has half the city pissed at her," his companion said cheerfully. "There's no need to worry about that." He rapped on the door, whispered a password to the guard, and ushered him into the darkness.

They hurried silently to the study and Orien went in first with a motion for him to stay back.

"I wondered where you had gone," Elantria said drily. "What happened?"

"Let's say anyone who trades in slaves has been extra jumpy lately," the elf said.

She sighed. "That *idiot*," she said with a sharp edge to her tone.

"Mmm, speaking of whom…" From the series of clanks and clicks, someone was picking the locks on his cuffs. "He's the reason I got out of there alive."

"What?" She had not seen that coming.

"Yes. You see, they brought me directly to Kerill and Birra for execution, and who should tumble out of the vault but Ben. Ah— that feels better, thank you." There was a last clank of iron on wood as the chains were put on the table, followed by the sound of wine being poured into a goblet. "He killed the guard holding me and threw his job to get me out."

"Really." Elantria sounded cautious.

"Mm-hmm. He's impulsive in both directions, as it turns out. But the point is, not only did he throw his job, he'd taken our advice to heart and planned to get Kerill's son into power instead of Birra."

"How did he plan to do that?"

"He can tell you himself." Orien raised his voice. "Ben."

"Oh, you have to be kidding me," she said as he came around the door.

"I'm afraid not." He managed a smile, although he was fairly sure it looked more like a grimace. "Trust me, I asked Orien numerous times if he was sure about this."

"Why were you in Kerill's vault?" she demanded. "Who hired you?"

Ben weighed the pros and cons of hiding the man's name and decided it was probably best for her to know. "Nemon. Through Delia."

"Ugh." Elantria flopped into her chair. "I don't know what Delia sees in him. What did he hire you for?"

"To get a necklace—an ugly old thing covered in jewels. He said no one had used it in a while and probably wouldn't even notice it was missing." He considered whether to sit or get himself a glass of wine and decided to do neither. He didn't want to piss her off.

What he wanted was to leave, but he wasn't sure he'd be able to do that.

"And…" The woman looked at Orien.

"And when we were surrounded, he yanked it out and threw it to distract them," the elf said.

"That was foolish," Elantria snapped.

"We didn't have very many choices. Would you rather Orien was dead?"

"No, but you could have left him to die."

"Yes, I could have done that at any point." He was getting angry now. "I didn't, though, which should tell you something about me."

"Mm." She didn't seem convinced.

"Look," the elf interjected. "I need to go get stitched up because the wound in my arm has opened again. And I need new clothes unless I want green things to grow in unpleasant places. I cannot leave, however, until you two promise not to kill each other while I am gone."

Elantria stared at him and he mirrored it. He looked at Ben, who also said nothing.

"I mean it," Orien said. He jabbed fingers at each of them. "Both of you, promise right now or I'll knock your heads together like coconuts."

She scowled. "I'll promise not to harm him," she said, "as long as he doesn't try to harm *me*."

"Or hurt," the elf said.

The woman glowered. "Or hurt," she conceded.

"Ben?"

He folded his arms, but it turned out that Orien could be quite imposing when he wanted to. "Fine. I won't harm—*or* hurt—her, as long as she doesn't try to harm me."

"Good enough." He smiled pleasantly at both of them. "If either of you breaks your promise, I *will* make sure you face justice, by the way."

"You'd sell me out for him?" Elantria asked and sounded almost offended.

"He saved my life. It would only be polite." Orien settled a stern look on each of them before he left.

Ben and Elantria stared at one another.

"You're an idiot," she said finally.

"That is debatable." He sighed. "But I have been informed that I should *not* have called you a coward, so…I apologize for that."

She folded her arms.

"You can change more than you give yourself credit for," he said fiercely.

That, oddly, was what broke her bad mood. She gave him a strange smile and sat in her chair near the fire with one boot propped on the other.

"You sound like Orien. That's probably why he likes you."

"I wouldn't go *that* far."

Now, Elantria grinned. "Fair enough." She leaned forward with her elbows on her knees. "Very well. I don't like you. It'll be a while before I can trust you again. But you can stay the night here. Go get some fresh clothes, too."

He hesitated. "Thank you," he said quietly.

The woman looked briefly at him and gave a tiny nod. She seemed as uncomfortable with apologies as he was.

That was at least a tiny kinship. He left her to her thoughts.

CHAPTER TWENTY-FIVE

"Okay, get ready!" Taigan sprinted through the tall grass, her staff at the ready. "There are three of them and they are *mega* pissed!"

Behind her, three jackalopes with glittering fur and very sharp teeth hopped heavily through the field. Very large rabbits, it turned out, were not as fast as the small ones.

That was the good part. The *bad* part was the fact that they hit like a goddamned train.

She burst out of the grass to where Jamie stood, still bent over, and panted from the last fight. "Ha! I can see you!"

"Yeah, crazy." He stood and hefted his sword. "And all it took was doing something monumentally stupid."

"This isn't *that* stupid." She took a position next to him and leveled her staff.

"You're right. Maybe next time, we should up the ante and jump off a cliff."

Taigan stuck her tongue out at her brother. Since they had found out that exposure to danger shifted her into his type of consciousness, they had maintained a fairly steady series of fights. At this rate, by sometime next week, there wouldn't be a single living animal on the island.

Prima had seen the direction this was going in and had moved them to this new zone before they did irreparable damage to the ecosystem.

They could first see the jackalopes as a rustle in the grass, then caught the occasional glimpse of antlers as they bounded along. When the three finally reached the clearing, she winced.

"Okay, I didn't realize quite how big they were."

"Those are *bears*," Jamie said. "Okay, they're jackalopes, but those are fucking *bear-sized*. What the fuck?"

"Sorry?" she ventured with a shrug and a pained grin. She whipped her staff onto the top of one creature's head when it crept closer with a growl. It yelped and backed away. "I'll take two. How about that?"

"Yeah, you'd fucking better!" He thrust his sword at one of the other two. "These freaking things. They know a sword isn't a good defense against them. Fuck, fuck, fuck, fuck—" He began to circle and stabbed with the sword again. This time, he caught the jackalope's nose. "Yeah, that's right, you bunny bitch."

"Mom is gonna wash your mouth out with soap," Taigan warned him. She swung the staff down to thump it on one animal's front paws and swept the point up to catch the other on the chin.

"If I can't swear when facing bear-sized bunnies, when *can* I?"

"You *know* her answer to that would be 'never,'" she retorted. Both her adversaries lunged toward her at the same time, and she jabbed the staff outward on instinct and held it horizontal so each end caught one of the jackalopes. It was probably the best thing she could have done, but the impact reverberated through her hands so hard that she yelped. "Ow, son of a—" She caught Jamie's interested look. "Bench," she finished.

"Come on, let it out." He flashed her a grin. "Swear it up. You *know* you want to. You can—ow, fuck! All right, bunny. Now, it's *personal.*" Immediately, he went on the offensive and drove forward with his left hand back. He had spent three years competing in fencing and the more tired he became, the more those instincts came out.

Taigan had to admit that fencing was an elegant and very civilized way to fight. That said, she also had to acknowledge that her fighting instincts weren't so much elegant as very smashy. She whirled and whacked both jackalopes across the face as she did so, brought the staff up over her head, and plunged it down like a spear on one of her opponent's head.

It collapsed like a sack of pink, glittery bricks.

"That'll teach *you* to chase someone halfway across a field." She panted and paused to regroup.

The other creature took the opportunity, launched forward, and landed on her shoulders. She fell with a shriek and in the next moment, a crushing weight settled on her back.

"These things are *heavy!*"

"*Bears,* Taigan. They're the size of bears!"

"Yeah, that's great and all, but maybe you could help?" She looked up and yelped when teeth snapped near her face. When she flailed her legs and arms, she managed to hit several soft areas but seemed not to have struck anything exceedingly tender given the limited range of her prone position.

She couldn't maneuver well enough to use the staff in her current position, nor could she turn with so much weight on her legs. Her best bet to avoid the teeth was most likely to stay in constant motion so she tried to push to her hands and knees and tucked her head in to avoid another snap of teeth. She jabbed her elbows back but found only air.

Shit.

With a yodel, Jamie came to the rescue. The jackalope screamed and scuttled sideways. He grabbed his sister's arm to haul her up and she snatched the staff up and immediately returned to the offensive. She drove the animal back with stabs and lunges with the weapon and finally managed to catch it in the eye.

A low growl issued from its throat. It was the only one left and its blood ran from one eye and the flank. Old blood on its teeth and antlers revealed that it was much more accustomed to winning than losing.

But it wasn't down yet and it was *pissed.*

The twins adjusted their hands around the grips of their weapons.

"Ready?" Taigan asked Jamie without looking at him.

"Ready." She could hear his grin and didn't need to look at him. "Operation Rock and a Pointy Place, Iteration 503."

"May we leave this island a barren wasteland," she said solemnly and tried not to let her mouth twitch.

They charged simultaneously with a yell. Taigan circled to the outside and whipped the staff to drive the jackalope away. It retreated with a hiss but its gaze was fixed on her.

Probably because she was screaming at the top of her lungs.

Operation Rock and a Pointy Place was the best tactic they had come up with thus far. She made herself impossible to ignore with many thwacks of the staff and a great deal of irregular screaming, caught the enemy's full attention, and drove them toward Jamie.

This one was canny, however. It refused to be driven straight back and instead, counter-circled to keep both of them in its line of vision.

"Clever girl," Jamie muttered.

"It has antlers, Jamie."

"It's a mythical animal, *Taigan.*"

"Fair point. Oh, for fuck's sake. Would you have the courtesy to *die?*" She uttered a frustrated ululation and thwacked her staff down as hard as she could. "What? Come on, jackalope. Come and get some!"

It accepted the challenge.

"Fuck!" She flung herself prone as the creature vaulted overhead and was already rolling to her feet when it landed. The flat of her staff caught it hard across the side and Jamie raced past to get behind it. "Operation Rock!" the girl yelled.

He put all his weight behind the stab. "And a pointy place," he finished, panting heavily. He stumbled forward and held his hand out to clasp hers.

Taigan laughed. "Based on how you look, I must look like total shit."

Her brother studied her. "Your hair has a certain…mad-scientist look to it." He held one finger up and began to gather her hair and lift it straight up. "Prima, can we try a mohawk on my sister?"

"Of course, Mr. Mattis." The AI's tone was a perfect parody of a personal assistant. *"Please stand by."*

"Prima!" the girl yelled. She was laughing, though.

Her hair raised on its own. She felt it with some trepidation but it was still soft, held in place by magic. It seemed to have been smoothed and straightened and was simply a foot-and-half-high arc across the top of her head.

"Well, it *feels* cool," she said. "How does it—"

She stopped. Her brother was doubled over and laughed silently. She folded her arms and stared as he looked up, caught sight of her hair, and collapsed into tears of laughter again.

"I hope you break a rib," Taigan said. "Prima, can we try pink hair on my brother?"

"Of course, Ms. Mattis. Please stand by."

"No!" Jamie gasped.

His protest came too late. His hair flickered from its usual black and burst into a profusion of fuchsia. How Prima had managed to intuit his least favorite of all the pinks, Taigan didn't know, but she had certainly exceeded all expectations.

"Thank you, Prima," she said sweetly.

She and Jamie stared at one another, she with her hair in an absurd and physics-defying mohawk, and he with his hair an improbably vivid pink.

A moment later, Taigan flickered out of existence.

"Dammit!" she said loudly. Capital letters on Jamie's whiteboard informed her that he'd said the same thing. "Okay, another set of jackalopes. Prima, don't let him change his hair."

"You should know he has requested that you also not be allowed to change yours."

"Could you make it blue?"

"One moment, Ms. Mattis. I will check... He says he will only settle for purple."

"Ugh, I hate purple. Never mind. Where are the nearest jackalopes?"

"I do not believe—"

Something stirred in her mind. It felt like a piece of wrinkled clothing or an itch in her throat. She shifted without realizing she was doing it and flickered into existence again.

"Ha!"

"Whoa!" Jamie, who had been trying to coat his pink hair in mud, jumped.

"Cheater," Taigan said in mock outrage. "Prima, add sparkly bows."

He sighed as several pink bows with rhinestones appeared in his hair. "Do I *want* to know what I look like?"

"No. You also don't want me to request pictures of this for when we get out—but I'm gonna do it." She gave him a double thumbs-up.

Her twin folded his arms. "How did you get back here, anyway?" he demanded. With half his hair pink, half covered in mud, and all of it decorated with bows, he didn't look very imposing—not that either twin was particularly overawed by the other one to start with.

"I second that question," Prima interjected.

"I'm...not sure." She frowned and thought through what had

happened. "It felt…uh, like scratching an itch, you know? I think maybe I've come in and out so many times that I know the feeling of it now. It's like…um…oh, focusing and unfocusing your eyes."

"Huh." Jamie studied her carefully. "Prima, can *you* see a difference?"

"Yes. I had hoped that these efforts would simply shift Taigan into the correct form of consciousness and had not considered the possibility that switching between the two would be a skill she could cultivate. From the available data, I believe this is an important change."

The siblings looked at each other for a moment and both shrugged. Neither was quite sure what to make of the science-speak, but everyone seemed to agree this was going well.

"Okay," Taigan said slowly. "So if I can keep myself in this plane of—oh, fuckity fuck." She could no longer see Jamie. "Sweet, fancy Moses on a log."

"I've never heard that one before."

"Yeah, well, buckle in, because you'll hear many more of those things if I can't find out how to shift—oh, hey." She smiled at her brother. "You're back. I'm back. Whatever."

"You'll use that to get out of conversations you're losing, won't you?"

"I have no idea what you mean," she said loftily. "So, Prima…can I…"

She suddenly felt a little dizzy. Had the solution always been there, simply waiting for this technology? Was she ready to open her eyes and wake up?

Prima guessed what she planned to ask. *"I'm afraid not,"* she said gently. *"You and Jamie now exist in the same dream state, but while he has to be held in that state artificially, you remain there."*

Taigan looked at the sky, then at Jamie. He came to stand near her, a comforting presence with ridiculous hair. She leaned her head on his shoulder and jerked away when he spluttered.

"Mohawk up my nose."

"Ewww." She brushed the top of her hair off, then sighed and grasped his hand. "So, Prima, what you're saying is you have no idea when I will wake up."

"Oh, not at all." The AI sounded surprised. *"Now, we find ourselves at the place I began at with Justin. We are in familiar territory to use the human expression."*

"Oh!" The girl had braced herself for another series of unknowns. "Wait, seriously?"

"Seriously." If Prima were human, she would have been smiling. *"I think it's time to return to the rest of the PIVOT world and begin your adventures."*

"Oh, my God." Taigan gave a disbelieving laugh and threw herself into Jamie's arms. "Oh, my God! Oh, my God. This is amazing."

He hugged her close. "This is amazing," he echoed. "We'll make this work. We'll do it."

It was only when she felt him shaking that she realized he was crying. *"Jamie?"*

"I was so scared," he whispered. "Every time. I was so scared we'd lose you. I would dream I was you and I couldn't wake up."

"You won't lose me." Her chin trembled. "Because you never stopped fighting. I hope I'll be worth it."

"Does that mean you'll let me take the bows out of my hair?" he asked hopefully.

"Fat chance."

CHAPTER TWENTY-SIX

Ben woke with the certainty of what he needed to do.

He pushed the covers back and swung his feet out of bed. This was a strange feeling. It wasn't the same as the usual, frenetic urgency he usually experienced that brought the inability to focus on anything except his current passion. This certainty sat bone-deep and it did not need his immediate action. It did not worry that he would forget about it.

Unfortunately, he was very sure Elantria and Orien wouldn't like it. He scratched his scalp and heaved a sigh.

"Is something wrong?"

"Not exactly." He explained what he was thinking.

"I have to say, I think it's a risky plan."

"I know." He shrugged. "The thing is, if I don't do it, I'll always regret it. I'm too quick to say I've missed my opportunity or messed everything up."

"Hmm."

"Any follow-up?"

"No. I'm thinking. I find I like the human convention of saying 'hmm' while I do so."

"Right." He put his clothes on and went to find Elantria. Much to his surprise, she and Orien were entertaining guests, both of whom looked at Ben when he walked into the room.

He stopped dead. "Nemon. Delia."

"Well, fancy that," Nemon said.

Elantria sighed. "Okay, fine. He *is* here."

"You lied for me?" He looked at her in surprise and smiled slightly. "Thank you."

She shrugged awkwardly. "I *told* you I didn't want your death on my conscience."

"She thought I intended to kill you," the man said. He managed to sound deeply injured at the mere insinuation. "Even when I told her I wasn't planning to do that."

"You aren't?" Despite his reservations, he smiled. He leaned on the table and regarded the visitors with at least a semblance of calm.

"Of course not. I haven't laughed as hard in months as I did when I heard what happened at the compound." He took a sip of coffee. "I only wish I'd been there to see Kerill's face when you fell out of the vault."

"And you're…not angry that I failed to get the artifact?" he asked cautiously.

"*This* artifact?" Nemon pulled the necklace out of a pocket in his vest.

"My gods," Orien said in something close to horror. "You weren't joking. That is as ugly as sin."

"Isn't it?" Ben grimaced.

The man turned it in his hands and assessed it critically. "I think it has a certain elegance."

"You think that because it's worth so much money, dear," Delia said with obvious fondness.

"Forget that. How did you *get* it?" Ben asked.

"I would hardly send an untried novice alone into one of the most well-guarded houses in Heffog," Nemon told him. Again, he sounded offended. "I make backup plans. You were not the only person there that night."

"Were you dressed as a guard?" he asked suspiciously.

Nemon smiled. "Not me, but you have the tactic right. It was very tragic, you know. The guards tried to decide between the escaped slave and the necklace and wound up with neither. Kerill was immensely displeased."

"How terrible for him," he muttered.

"I don't think you mean that."

"You're right, I don't." He considered the necklace. "Well, that makes my plan somewhat simpler, then. I thought Kerill would keep an eye on that piece in particular for a while. But, since he's not—"

"Ben," Elantria interjected with impressive restraint, "what *exactly* are you planning?"

"Well." He smiled around the room. "I want to assassinate Kerill and Birra, and I would guess you two wanted to rob him blind, yes? And Nemon would certainly love to get his hands on a few more pieces. So…what do you all say we do that?"

"*What?*" she demanded.

Nemon burst out laughing. "He's going in again. Ah, the stones on this one. I should associate with more humans. They always surprise me." He took Delia's hand and kissed the back of it and she smiled at him.

Elantria met Ben's gaze over their heads and shrugged as if to say she still didn't understand the couple.

He thought he did. Whatever else he was, the man was charming and he delighted in flouting social norms, much in the same way Delia seemed to. Both were tolerant of each other's foibles.

"So, you are going back?" Elantria asked him.

"I am. I came up with a damned good plan the first time and I intend to follow through." He folded his arms and looked at each of them. "Not that anyone else has to get involved, but it *would* help."

"You don't say." She sighed. "And then you'd involve me—publicly—in another assassination."

Rather than reply, he waited. His instinct was to blabber about how important this was, but he had the good sense to keep his mouth shut. He studied the emotions that flitted across her face.

"I don't like this turning into outright war," she admitted. She seemed to be talking to the fireplace.

"You knew it was coming, though," Orien said.

She looked sharply at him. "I did not. How would I know that?"

"Because whenever there's mass enslavement, there's a war," he said bluntly. "You helped me escape and you've helped others. You've targeted slave traders for a while now. And while you were getting ready for something bigger, I…"

Elantria looked at him in surprise and waited for him to finish the sentence.

"I was gathering information," the elf said. "I told myself the delay was good but I was too much of a coward to make it a war." Wryly, he said to Ben, "When I told you not to call her a coward, it was because I knew which of the two of us deserved that title."

"We can all share it," Nemon said equably.

Everyone looked at him.

"I thought that might move the conversation along." He raised an eyebrow. "No? Well, then. Regardless, an attack on Kerill *would* make a good opening salvo in a war."

"What do you know of war?" Elantria asked bluntly.

"I know showmanship," he said with a flourish of one hand. "You and I both know that elves like to dress up their brutishness with pretty words, but the one thing they respect is a show of force. Kerill was allowed to do what he did because no one opposed him. The question here is whether we go with the original plan or we do this openly."

Utter silence followed his challenge.

Ben considered what he'd heard for a moment and then, tired of his butt going numb while he propped himself on the table, dragged a chair to the fire and sat with the others.

"So, it's a question of trying to make it fall apart without them knowing," he said, "or doing it in the open." The others nodded. "There would be less pushback if it's quiet, I guess," he mused. "But we run the risk of it simply going elsewhere. There's no possibility that it would all fall apart without Kerill, I guess."

"Now that there's a profit being made, it's not likely." Elantria sighed.

"Actually, depending on how we did it…" Orien frowned in thought. "He sold me knowing I was elven and of his same nation. It's against elven law. I'd be within my rights to kill him."

"What are you saying?" She looked warily at him.

"I'm saying that if the rest of you hold the guards off, I could make his death a symbol." His face was like a mask now. "I don't have redress against his heir, but—"

"I could handle that," Ben said quietly. "Then the estate would pass to his son. Elven slave traders would be shamed, and—"

"And the trade begins to fall apart in Heffog," Elantria murmured. "We'd need to be careful to prevent the humans from sweeping in and filling the gap in the market."

"I think you're forgetting that you're known as Jorys' assassin." Nemon raised his eyebrows at her. "That was rather a sign of things to come, wasn't it?"

"Ah. Right." She looked sourly at Ben, although there was amusement there. "I keep forgetting how my reputation has changed in the past few days."

"I don't think you forget anything ever," Ben retorted. A smile tugged at his lips. "In fact, I anticipate reminders of this for the rest of my natural life assuming you don't shorten that span yourself."

"A good caveat," she said blandly.

He smiled and shifted in his chair.

"Are you well, Ben?" Nemon asked. "You have a strange look on your face."

"I'm, uh…" Feeling had begun to come back and half his butt experienced pins and needles. "It's nothing." Trying not to leap out of his chair and wiggle around the room, he returned to the subject at hand. "So, Orien kills Kerill while the rest of us hold the guards off —if necessary—and I kill Birra. Orien then, presumably, makes some kind of public statement—"

"I have to make the accusation first," the elf said and sighed. "There have to be witnesses. I'll need seven heads of household to watch. They don't all have to be noble, which makes it easier, but it does remove the element of surprise somewhat."

"Only somewhat?" Ben quipped. "So holding the guards off will be imperative. Okay."

"And you or Delia will need to kill Birra," Nemon told him. "Orien is right. He has no redress there. Anyone with elven blood will be held to elven law as soon as it's invoked."

"I can do it," Delia said. "I can get into any noble house."

"No." Ben shook his head. "This is your city and you're known to be close to Nemon. You don't need to risk it. I'm an outsider so I *can* take the risk. When this is over, I'll disappear."

"You have to get through it alive first, smart guy."

Ben smiled slightly, knowing the others in the room wouldn't have heard the joke. Oddly, this was what gave him the most confidence in the plan working out. Prima would never joke if she were truly worried. She had reminded him to be careful but at the same time, she told him she thought it was possible.

"I can't decide if I'd rather you stay here," Elantria murmured, "or whether I'd rather set you loose without any idea which city you would set on fire next."

"Hey." He rolled his eyes. "I've grown up considerably since the start of this. In the future, any violence will be precisely targeted and considered in advance."

"You say that like it's comforting," she replied waspishly.

"She's right, you know. It's not comforting at all."

He threw his hands up. "Fine. Everyone else come up with the plan and I'll go along with it. Promise."

"It's a solid plan," Nemon said. "I don't think we need to alter it much. I, however, must move quickly to find the seven heads of household to serve as witnesses. It's not essential that they be sympathetic to our cause, but I think we can all agree that this isn't time to push the odds out of our favor."

He disappeared and Delia bent to murmur a few words in Orien's ear before she followed.

"What did she say?" Ben asked when she was gone. "Never mind. If she'd wanted the rest of us to hear—"

"It's fine." Orien looked even paler than usual. "She told me that there is a reason elven law sentences slave traders to death. Delia knows how much I've doubted this and in fact, she told me to do it immediately after my escape." He saw Ben's surprise. "Nemon and Delia took me in originally when I escaped and Elantria helped me from there."

"So the four of you go way back," He said.

"You could say that." The elf nudged Elantria with an elbow. "And they've only tried to kill each other a few times. Come on now, we need to do some planning."

The two of them hurried away as well and left him seated alone on his chair.

"That was a joke," he called after them. "Right? Guys?"

There was no answer.

"People in this city are insane," he told Prima.

"Maybe that's why you fit in so well."

CHAPTER TWENTY-SEVEN

Once the decisions were made, Elantria and Nemon both swung into action with impressive speed.

Runners were dispatched from her house and within the hour, dozens of people appeared. At first glance, they looked wildly different—children, stooped old women, fishermen, and serving girls in livery. As often as not, however, a disguise fell away to reveal an entirely different shape beneath, and whether or not they were in disguise, all of them had watchful eyes and weapons.

Elantria summoned them to a meeting in the early afternoon. Instead of in the courtyard, which Ben had expected, it was held in the basement. He walked past a confusingly large pile of crates in the main hall and down the stairs to where dozens of pairs of eyes all focused on him mistrustfully.

"This is Ben," she said and gestured at him. "You'll know him as Jorys' assassin."

The mistrust grew somewhat less palpable.

"Tonight," she said, "Ben will deal with Birra and her guards. Kule, Havern, I want you to go with him. Raise your hands so he knows who you are."

Two people complied. He could not have said at a glance whether they were elven, human, dwarven, or a mixture of all three. Both were slight and short, with dark hair and dusky skin. Something was unsettling about how dark their eyes were, and it took him a moment to notice what.

They had no whites. Every part of the orb was black.

Ben swallowed, nodded, and decided not to ask questions about that. He was half-sure they might be actual demons and he didn't want to learn too much and wind up dead.

"Promise you'll yank me out of this world if they try to possess me," he muttered under his breath as he and Orien tramped down the last couple of creaking stairs.

"Awwww, you're no fun."

He leaned against the back wall with his arms folded and made a point of not looking at Kule and Havern.

"As you know, we will move against Lord Kerill tonight." Elantra looked at her team. "He is the architect of the slave trade in Heffog and his death will be a symbol. Many of you know Orien." She gestured to him. "As an elf of the same nation, he has the right under elven law to kill Kerill for his crimes. Tonight, he will do so."

A murmur swelled through the gathering.

"What changed?" Kule asked the question, or possibly Havern. Ben could not have said for sure if the one who spoke was male or female. The voice clarified nothing. It seemed to be an entirely normal voice, but…things…lurked in it.

Things with teeth, his imagination said. The back of his neck crawled.

Elantria looked at the two demons—he had decided to think of them as demons—and considered her words carefully.

"I'll let Ben answer that," she said finally.

He gaped at her in surprise.

She gestured for him to come forward. The gleam in her eyes said that this was a little payback for bringing her into this situation. *You started this,* her smile said. *Now you have to make the speeches.*

Ben swallowed. He walked to the table where she had spread her documents and looked at the crowd. An unsettling number of those present had eyes of unrelieved black. He saw elves and dwarves and even someone who looked as if they might have orc blood. Heffog truly was a melting pot.

"What changed is that I killed Jorys," he said abruptly after a moment. "It was a stupid decision and there was no plan. I saw the opportunity and I took it, and I put Elantria in danger—and all of you, I suppose. I want you to know that she would have been more cautious with this. Anyone who knows her probably won't be surprised to hear that she read me the riot act and threw me out on my ass."

This triggered a burst of surprised laughter. He looked at Elantria and she smiled slightly.

"But my stupidity doesn't end there," he said to another round of laughter. "Because after I did that and she chewed me out, I decided to *argue* with her. Now, for those of you wondering how I'm still alive, I have no idea so I can't answer you."

There was a snicker from nearby. Orien had his face buried in one hand and his shoulders shook with laughter.

"Well, the long story short is that both Elantria and I made some good points in that argument." He smiled at them. "All of you know that she'd do almost anything to keep the people in this city safe. I'm too impulsive, and she was…maybe a little too cautious."

He met her gaze and waited for her tiny nod. She made him wait but she smirked a little.

"And she listened to a few of us," he continued, "when we suggested that now might be the time to strike. Kerill has been unopposed for years while he turned Heffog into a trading hub for slaves, but it's time to end it. We all agreed on that. In the end…the rest was merely details."

At his gesture, Elantria returned to the table. "It's a close enough rendition of the facts," she said and provoked another round of chuckles. "We have allies in this fight. Over the years, the underworld of Heffog has grown strong. We are many and the nobles are few."

"You're a noble," said someone. They didn't seem overawed by her at all.

Ben couldn't imagine that.

"I have noble blood," she corrected. "As does Nemon. So we can both tell you how little that's worth and how good they are at making rules to ensure that only a few people claim the title. With many of their number gone to join the elven monarchy, the rest are weak. They sought to consolidate power and rule us through fear, but that won't work. Not anymore. Jorys was the first. Kerill and his niece are next. From there…we will see where it goes."

"A bloodbath," Prima said dryly. *"That's the expression, isn't it?"*

He nodded.

"Are you sure you don't want to stay and help them with that?"

"I'm better for the first part," he murmured. "But I'll consider it."

Elantria called various people to the table to give them their assignments and most left at a run. Kule and Havern stayed close, their gazes fixed on Ben each time he looked up.

When there were only a few left, she looked at Orien.

"Are you ready?" she asked him.

He looked thoughtful. "No. But I never will be." He managed a smile. "He destroyed us. He scattered us across the world and sold our lives for a pile of gold coins he didn't even need." His gaze hardened and settled on her. "I told you the first time we met that this was coming. Then, I hid from it."

"And I let you." She smiled sadly in return. "Until someone gave us a push."

Both looked at Ben, who cleared his throat awkwardly.

Elantria focused on the elf again. "Kerill had already planned a dinner tonight and had invited three heads of household. There will be three more in the building from common-born families, and one more noble he was able to convince to drop by. You'll have your seven witnesses.'

"Thank you." Orien nodded. "I'll…go get ready."

She watched him walk away with a small frown, then said to Ben, "Watch out for him."

"I will."

"Remember." Her face was grave. "He *must* be the one to kill Kerill. Keep him safe but do not finish the job for him."

He nodded. "I'll deal with Birra as quickly as I can and get back to him."

"Good." She nodded to him, and to Kule and Havern. "Go with the gods. Strike swiftly and true. Your carriage is upstairs."

Ben had questions about how they were supposed to get past the guards, but those were answered immediately once he got upstairs. The carriage, which waited out front, was half-full and being loaded.

It wasn't so much a carriage, however, as a cart.

The conveyance was full of crates.

He sighed. Now he understood why all those crates were there. He was supposed to get into one, wasn't he? It seemed all kinds of disappointing that he would be smuggled into Kerill's house like a sack of potatoes.

The discomfort of that idea was vastly increased when he realized he would be shut in with the two demons.

"You have to be kidding me," he whispered to Prima as Kule and Havern climbed into the crate.

"If you don't want to get shut in crates with demons, don't start civil wars."

"Ah, yes, the old saying. Now I remember." He glared at the sky before he stepped into the crate. The lid came down immediately and he was alone in the dark with the two demons, neither of whom seemed to be breathing.

This was normal, he told himself. It wasn't at all worrisome.

"So…how did you come to work with Elantria?" Ben asked.

A hissing sound unnerved him until he realized it was a laugh.

"She hired us for a job," said one of them. "An impossible job for one of the mortal races. She had a hunch after it about what we were, so she got us drunk and talked our real names out of us."

"I…" Ben had not anticipated this.

"She doesn't hurt us," one of them said. "She merely bound us to an oath to not hurt any of the mortals in the city."

Both made disappointed hissing noises.

He didn't know what to say to that, especially since he was shut in a crate with them. "Ah," he said finally.

Both burst out laughing at that.

"We're kidding," one of them said.

"We're dark elves," the other added.

"There aren't many of us," said the first.

"Everyone gets freaked out about our eyes," the second concluded.

Ben sighed.

"Oh, come on," his partner said. "We don't get a chance to freak new people out very often."

"Yeah, yeah." He tried to ignore the sound of Prima laughing in his head.

The trip to Kerill's house lasted longer than he would have liked. The two elves seemed content to wait in silence and made no complaint when the heat began to build. Neither seemed to get motion sick in the carriage, either, which he certainly did.

Eventually, the cart was unloaded, which was even worse. He braced himself while the crate was hauled into someplace dark and blessedly cool.

"Now what?" he asked as quietly as he could.

"Now we wait for nightfall," said one of them.

"Kerill was expecting a shipment of rare artifacts from the fae lands," said the other.

"Elantria has those now."

"And instead, Kerill has a warehouse full of enemy soldiers," Ben finished before the other one could. "Not bad. She must be rather pleased with herself."

"Probably," said one of them. They sounded sulky that he hadn't let them finish their game of imparting wisdom as a pair.

The hours ticked past interminably. There was nothing to do except stretch at various intervals to stop his muscles from cramping, but the activity didn't do much at this juncture. By the time he heard rustling around them, he ached all over and he almost leapt out of the box when the lid was removed.

Everyone eased stiff muscles and shared a light meal, but his heart beat wildly. He almost wasn't able to eat.

"*Are you well?*" Prima enquired worriedly.

"I think so," he murmured. "But I'm usually gone by this point. You know, the fight. Once I've stirred things up."

"*Would I be correct in assuming that once you leave this game, you'll have rather a lot of apologies to make?*"

He sighed. "Yes."

"*Mmm. Well, good luck with that.*"

"Thanks." He looked around, located Kule and Havern, and jerked his head at them.

It was time to go before he could think better of this crazy plan he'd set in motion.

CHAPTER TWENTY-EIGHT

Amber was several hours deep in one of her spreadsheets when Nick came to find her. He waved a cup of fresh coffee under her nose until she looked up blearily.

"Hey, do you have a sec?"

"What's up?" She removed her earbuds.

"Ben's friends are calling in a few minutes about his progress. I thought it might be good to have us on the call as well as DuBois."

"Oh." She took her ponytail out hastily and combed her hair back slightly more neatly. "Sure. Thanks for the coffee. What time is it?"

"Almost noon."

"Oh." She yawned as she followed him through the lab toward the hall to the conference room. "Oof. It's been a long morning."

"Yeah, when did you come in?"

She decided to drink her coffee instead of answering and hoped he wouldn't notice.

"Amber?" He raised an eyebrow.

"Four AM. Give or take." She shrugged. "I had an idea and then I couldn't let it go, so I came in."

"You woke at four AM with an idea about accounting?" Nick asked skeptically.

"I was already up."

"Why were you—" He broke off at the slight smile on her face. "Never mind, *don't* tell me. I can fill in the blanks. Although I have to say, getting an idea about spreadsheets during *that* is worse than waking up with one."

"That wasn't what gave me the idea," she protested, laughing.

"Uh-huh. Sure. Do you two dirty talk by saying excel formulas at each other, or what?"

Amber gave up on trying to drink coffee through her laughter. "Well, not *only* that. We also recite obscure parts of the US Tax Code to each other."

He mimed fanning himself. "We shouldn't talk about this at work."

The two friends were still laughing when they entered the room to see that the video call had already started. They shut up hastily and waved at the two people on the screen.

"These are my colleagues," Dr. DuBois said.

"Hi, I'm Amber," she said with a wave.

"And I'm Nick," he added. "We're two of the three founders of PIVOT."

"Nice to meet you," said the woman on the screen. She had wildly curly hair and a slim, lanky frame. "I don't know if you remember me. I'm Natasha, and this is my fiancé, Mike."

The man beside her managed a weak wave of one arm. His skin was pale and he seemed to have lost a great deal of muscle recently, but he looked miles better than he had the first time they had seen him. Most of the casts had been removed and they could see crutches and a wheelchair in the background.

"Of course we remember you." Nick smiled. "Mr. Parker, you're looking very well."

The man grimaced. "Thanks."

His companion smiled sympathetically at him. "Physical

Therapy isn't exactly a walk in the park," she explained, "and it's hard to miss a whole summer of climbing and surfing and all that. But he's recovering so well—much better than the doctors thought he would."

"They only say that so I feel special," Mike muttered, clearly in bad humor.

"I wouldn't be so sure," Amber told him. "Because they've been flabbergasted by Ben, and if the two of you are best friends, I'd bet you're equally stubborn."

Both Mike and Natasha laughed.

"I refuse to incriminate myself," the man said, "but I *will* throw Ben under the bus. He's a stubborn son of a bitch."

His fiancée pointed at him and mouthed, "He is, too."

Amber and Nick nodded.

"Wait, what did you say to them?" Mike demanded.

"Nothing," Natasha said innocently.

"Uh-*huh*." He narrowed his eyes. "Anyway. We were wondering what Ben's progress looked like for the wedding."

"We know you might not be able to tell us," the woman said.

"Ah…actually, Ben authorized us to share his progress with you." Amber smiled. "He said that either of you would be a better resource for bouncing treatment ideas off than his parents."

"Awkward," Mike said, "but not wrong. I hope you're able to at least *share* information with his parents."

"We are and I promise they haven't been in the dark this whole time."

"Whew," he said. "Okay, so how *is* he doing?"

"Well," DuBois said readily, "his manual dexterity has increased greatly within the game, as well as him mastering more precise movements. He has also been able to approximate rock climbing, though there appears to be a certain amount of trauma associated with that."

Mike's face was strained as he nodded. "I can imagine."

Natasha put her hand over his and they looked at each other for a moment.

"The good news is that he's been able to work through it," Nick said and cleared his throat awkwardly. "I wouldn't say it's gone by any stretch of the imagination, but he's doing well. As you said, he's a stubborn son of a bitch."

The man laughed at that and some of the tension in his shoulders eased. He swallowed before he asked, "And how is he emotionally? I don't want to be an asshole but I was very worried by how he was talking the last time he came out."

"Ah." The two engineers exchanged a look.

DuBois munched popcorn with a bemused expression on his face.

"Um…" Amber marshaled her thoughts. "Video games offer a unique opportunity to watch moral choices play out without affecting people. Of course, the resemblance to real life can be debated but they tend to be very impactful on an emotional level."

"Again, not to be an ass, but…that sounds like a long way of saying nothing." Mike shrugged and winced. "My shoulders don't like doing that yet."

Amber hesitated for a moment before she continued. "I don't want to betray any confidences," she said finally. "While Ben did authorize us to speak to you about medical issues, I think discussing particulars of his mental health would be crossing a line. With that said, I want to assure you that I am not worried at present. He seems to be in a very stable place. I…hope that helps. A little."

"So, without specifics," Natasha said before her fiancé could speak, "there's nothing for us to actively worry about at this time."

"In my opinion, no. Ben seems to be happy, shows social engagement, and copes well with complex emotional situations. I think I'm veering into specifics again." She cut herself off by taking a long swallow of coffee.

"I can…work with that." Mike sighed. "I want my friend back, you know? Him, not someone else."

"He's still him," Amber said.

He nodded.

"And you think he might be able to come out for the wedding?" Natasha asked them.

"With several stipulations," Nick said before DuBois could respond. "They would want two members of medical staff on-hand with him and he must *not* be asked to stand for more than five minutes at a time. I wouldn't plan to involve him in any ceremony over half an hour or so."

To his surprise, the woman pumped her fist in victory. "Oh, yeah. *Awesome.*"

"You'll want some context," Mike said. "My fiancée is not a complete bitch, I promise."

"Only mostly," she said with a grin. "No, it's only that my family has pressed for a huge wedding with a super elaborate ceremony and now, we can go, 'no, we really can't, it would be too much for Ben, doctor's orders.'" She began to chair-dance.

Her fiancé laughed silently in the background. He shook his head and shrugged.

"Don't you shake your head at me," she said. "You don't want to stand up for a long ceremony either."

"I said we should elope to New York," he pointed out.

"Oh!" DuBois looked happy. "Oh, that would be much better."

Natasha opened her mouth, then closed it.

"Think about it." Mike leaned close to her. "No sisters bitching about their bridesmaid gowns…no mothers trying to get pictures…"

"I feel like we shouldn't be here for this," Nick muttered. He and Amber averted their eyes hastily, although the doctor continued to watch with interest.

"I don't know," Natasha said.

"Everyone already has their flights on standby," he pointed out. "We can afford to lose the deposits. Come on, I saw you staring at the stack of wedding papers yesterday and you *know* you didn't look like you were looking forward to doing that paperwork."

"I wasn't. I'm not." She looked at him. "But can we do that? Like, can we truly do that?"

"We can do anything we want," he told her. "We can go to the greatest city on earth, see the Empire State Building—"

"Boy, do *you* know the way to a girl's heart." She laughed. "But…oh, my God, that sounds so much better than a big wedding. How mad do you think they'd be if we did this?"

"We could turn our phones off," Mike suggested. "And then we won't know."

"*Deal*," she said instantly. She swung to look at the camera. "We'll be there tomorrow. Does tomorrow work?"

DuBois and Amber looked at Nick, who nodded. "We can have him out by tomorrow."

"Awesome." Natasha smiled. "Okay, I have to handle…so many things."

"We have rooms available at one of the hotels near us," Nick said. "We have enough people flying in from out of town that we always have them. Let me check their availability and I'll send you an email."

"Holy crap, really?"

"It's much cheaper than us sending Ben cross-country with a full medical team," he pointed out.

"Oh. Um… Okay."

They said their goodbyes and hung up and he stretched luxuriously. "Working with a real *budget*? This is the *life*."

Amber shook her head and smiled, then yawned again. "Okay, I'll go home and sleep. Can you take care of the details for

Natasha and Mike? And text Jacob that they're coming into town and to pull Ben out?"

"Uh-huh." Nick nodded. "Go. Rest. I'll arrange it and see if I can't get another surprise in the works for Ben too."

"What were you thinking?"

"You'll see. Go rest." He smiled.

"Right." She yawned and headed out of the room. "Oooof, I'm tired. Oh, and text the doctors to come in for another assessment of Ben's—"

"I swear to God I will crush drugs up and put them in your coffee if you don't get out of here."

"Point taken." She snatched her coat and headed out.

CHAPTER TWENTY-NINE

Ben had memorized the layout of the entire compound while he was closed inside, waiting for the first heist. Now, he led Kule and Havern unerringly across the warren of streets and alleys that made up the outer edge of the location.

It was truly incredible how rich the nobles of this city were. Kerill practically commanded an entire city of his own, with livestock and metalsmithing as well as a veritable army of servants.

Those servants, if they noticed the sudden influx of people, took no notice. Despite the late hour, people trudged past with packages or handcarts. Some made their way wearily into the apartments that lined the outer wall.

He looked over his shoulder once and saw the flash of Orien's hair in the fading light. The half-elf walked straight-backed and dignified. He watched him for a moment and knew he did not envy him at all in this moment. The man joked and made a point of looking forward instead of back, but he also had the memory of being bought and sold—not to mention learning he was destined to die in an arena.

Now he was about to confront the man who had done it.

It was important to make sure Orien's courage meant something. When this was over, he couldn't let the elf feel as if this had been for nothing. He had to make sure the way was paved for a better city. He remembered the dwarf in Jorys' study and felt a simmering rage ignite in his chest.

This would end. He would end it himself, dammit.

They entered the main building via a passage that Nemon had marked on one of the maps. However the man had learned of it, it pained him to share the information, yet he had done so. The tunnel ran from the buttery on the eastern side of the mansion and directly into the kitchens.

Kule and Havern stepped aside to wait in the shadows outside the kitchens, while Ben adjusted his disguise and poked his head in.

"The Lady Birra—a man sent a message for Lord Kerill but said I was only to tell him if the lady *wasn't* there. Is she at dinner with the lord?"

The servants exchanged a glance.

"We're only cooks," a heavy-set man said gruffly. "We don't know a thing about what goes on upstairs."

They clearly knew something and he was interested to find out exactly what. He cast a glance over his shoulder as if to check for eavesdroppers and crept closer.

"Is it happening now?"

The servants all stopped and a couple of them leaned closer.

"Is *what* happening now?" one of them asked.

"He said it'd be tonight," he said, speaking of the fictitious event with the most conviction he could manage. "He said there would be a whole hue and cry about it. If it's happening now, he needs to know what I have to say."

The servants looked at each other and he saw their pleasure.

They hated Birra, as far as he could see. Whatever he was insinuating about a rift between Kerill and his heir, they were eager to see it happen.

"She's not at the dinner," one of them whispered. "She went snooping and she's in his study."

"What?" Ben drew a sharp breath and put on an appropriately outraged face.

"Whatever 'is lordship is planning, she seems to have guessed," another cook said. "'Ey, Yamira, any chance of sneaking a bottle of wine out of the cellars? I'm guessin' there'll be goodly gossip tonight."

The cook shushed them but everyone's eyes were alight with anticipation.

"As long as she's not at dinner, I can deliver the message," he said. "Thank you—and if you ever come by the Howling Coyote, drinks are on me."

They cheered at that and he stepped out into the hallway. Birra was alone in the study. This was the best way he could have hoped for this to go.

"What's a coyote?" Kule asked as they hurried through the mansion.

"It's a...wolf-thing. Kind of." He shook his head. "How many of them do you think will be out searching for that bar tomorrow night?"

"All of them," Havern guessed with a grin. "And it's too bad it doesn't exist because the gossip from tonight will be *legendary*."

Ben was still grinning when they came around the corner and saw Birra's guards waiting at the door of the study.

He didn't hesitate. If he did, the guards would gain the advantage and it would go poorly. He might have done some training with swords, but these men had trained for most of their lives.

As he pushed into a sprint toward them, he drew his short-sword, then threw himself into a roll. His pacing was good and he came out of it behind the far guard as the man staggered forward. He had drawn his sword to counter his attacker's swing and had thus leveled a heavy strike at thin air.

A little unbalanced by the futile attempt, he didn't have a

chance for another strike. Ben stabbed into the man's back and winced at his scream. He'd become better at steeling himself to the task of fighting, but it wasn't easy to see death up close.

Why couldn't he have been a virtual reality plumber, hopping over mushrooms and snagging gold coins? That would have been much less traumatic.

Right now, though, there was no time for regrets. The man staggered away and Ben arced his blade down for a final strike. On the other side, the two dark elves dispatched the second guard with silent efficiency. They fought in the same way they talked—one of them started an attack and the second finished it.

His guard made one last attempt at an attack, and he hit the man on the head with the hilt of his sword. He shuddered as he dropped like a stone. Even now, after all that had happened, he hated this.

Common sense reminded him that he had to stay alert. Birra was inside the study. He nodded at his companion and flung the door open.

A third guard stood inside, something he had anticipated. She seemed like the type to have increased her guard since the first time she'd encountered him. He wondered if she remembered him at all. The right side of his chest certainly remembered her. The colorful imprint of several diamonds still bruised the skin.

Kule and Havern moved to secure Birra while he and her bodyguard fought. He was powerfully built and imposing, definitely with orcish blood, and he moved like his massive broadsword weighed nothing.

The man was also tall, which meant he didn't bring his guard down quite enough. Ben parried several of his strikes, drove him back, and then—when the woman's scream distracted him—ducked low and stabbed up under the man's leather armor. A second slash followed across his throat and he stumbled upright to see Birra watching him.

"*You*," she said with undisguised hatred.

She *did* remember him. It would seem having a grimy human tackle you from behind what you thought was a solid wall was a formative experience.

"Me," he said cheerfully.

"What do you want?" she snapped. "Do you want another piece of treasure from my uncle's vault? Perhaps you want a bag of gold?"

"I came to kill you," he said.

"As you can see, my uncle isn't *here*," Birra snapped at him.

"Yes," he said patiently. "I know that. I said I came to kill *you*."

Her face paled and her mouth opened. She looked at Kule and Havern.

"What did my cousin pay you?" She was on her feet in a second. "I'll triple it. You'll be a rich man all your life—and that's before you get the payout for murdering him."

"Your cousin didn't send me," Ben told her.

She went even paler at that. "My uncle?" Her voice wavered now.

"It wouldn't be *that* much of a surprise, right? After all, you're spying on him while he's at dinner, he's been trying to get his son to come back as his heir…" He shrugged.

"Whatever you want," the woman said. "Name it and it is yours." Her gaze was cold. She was the type of person who was used to bending the world to her will. "Everyone has a price. Simply name yours."

"I want my father back, you son of a bitch."

"I…beg your pardon?" She looked at Kule and Havern, both of whom shrugged.

"It's a long story." Ben hefted his sword. "The short version is that there's no price that will stop this. You're dead, Birra."

"Why?" She spread her palms on the desk. "If it's not one of them, then *who*?"

He was torn. On the one hand, he didn't want to make the mistake of destroying his advantage with a speech. On the other, he wanted her to die knowing exactly what had led to her death.

"You destroyed lives," he said as he had to Jorys. "No amount of your pain could ever make that right—which is lucky for you. But you won't get out of this alive."

Her mouth opened on a denial and her scream was cut short when he vaulted over the desk to run her through. He didn't bother trying to cut through her jewel-encrusted dress but lunged at her throat. She died with a hidden dagger falling from one hand. Whether she had meant to kill him with it or herself, he didn't know.

He *did* know that there was another battle happening, and it was the more important one.

"Let's go," he said to his companions.

"But the vault is right there," Havern argued.

"*Now*, unless you want to explain to Elantria why we weren't there for Orien."

They shut up immediately and followed him without another word of protest. Elantria apparently inspired terror in her followers, even those who liked her.

They ran through silent hallways toward the sound of yells from the great hall. There were armed people inside, and he motioned for the other two to stay back while he peeked in one of the doors.

Kerill's guards had arrived too late. Orien and his fighters had Kerill surrounded, while seven elves stood along one side of the room. Three of them looked outraged, as did the slaver. The lord's guards didn't know what to do. They didn't dare get closer while the elf had their employer at knifepoint, and they didn't want to get involved in the workings of elven law either.

Ben motioned for Kule and Havern to follow him as he circled the outside of the great hall. He wanted to be quick but he couldn't afford anyone to hear them. Various phrases could be caught through the wall.

It turned out that legalese in elvish sounded very similar to legalese in English.

The three entered through the back door of the room in a rush to join Orien, who looked gratefully at them. The elf raised an eyebrow as if to confirm that his mission was accomplished.

He nodded.

"You have admitted to selling slaves," Orien said and returned to the matter at hand. "You have admitted, in front of witnesses, to selling *me*—a resident of your same city. You have admitted, also, to training me for purposes that would lead to my death. You are in violation of elven law."

Kerill looked desperately over his shoulder at the seven assembled elves. The four who had been called in by Nemon met his gaze without flinching. The man had known how they would see this.

The other three wouldn't look at the accused.

"You know this isn't a legal proceeding," Kerill called to them. His voice was high and wild.

"There are no protestations of innocence, you notice," Orien said clearly to no one in particular. "And you can save your breath. We can carry out the sentence before your guards can reach us."

The guards looked less and less sure of what they should be doing.

"Slavery has never been prohibited in Heffog," Kerill snapped at them. "*Do* something."

One of the men took a step forward miserably, and Orien's sword flashed. It came to rest along the lord's neck.

The man glared at him. "You'll never get out of here alive. They'll kill you as soon as you kill me."

"I don't think that's true," the ex-slave said. "After all, they have several noble witnesses who declare me to be in the right. They know you've claimed exemptions from other laws due to your adherence to elvish custom, which means you should hold to it now." He cast a speculative look at the guards. "And frankly, I don't think they care that much. Once you're dead, I don't think they'll risk their lives to fight my soldiers."

Kerill snarled at him. "What do you want? Is it money? A mansion of your own?"

"No," Orien said. He shook his head slightly at Ben. "They always offer the same things. They think it solves all their problems."

His mouth twitched.

"Then how about this?" Kerill's voice dropped and he suddenly had a smile on his lips. "I have records of where every slave was sent to. Everyone…including your friend Josyla."

The elf froze.

"Orien?" Ben asked quietly.

"They were rather more than friends," Kerill said. He sounded smug now and could see victory within his grasp. "I would have kept them together but you see, she fetched quite a good price as a goldsmith—and why keep her here, only to see him die in the arena? But now that he's free…"

He could see that it cost the slave trader, even now with his actual life on the line, to say goodbye to the money he'd received for Josyla.

"A deal could be made," he finished.

Ben watched Orien's indecision and fought the urge to run Kerill through himself. He didn't believe that Josyla was still alive. The man couldn't be trusted at all. It was merely an attempt to weasel out of this.

But this was exactly what Elantria had worried about. It was why she had warned him that Orien *must* be the one to kill Kerill. He had a thought, suddenly, of exactly how to ensure that.

He stepped close to Orien to murmur in his ear. "When this is over—immediately after you do what you came here for—I'll need to leave Heffog. Send me to look for Josyla. Between Kerill's records and my…magical spirit…we'll find her and we'll free her.

Don't let him weasel out of paying for this simply for Josyla's sake. We can have both."

The elf looked at him. "And I suppose he might be lying." His jaw was tight.

"Then he *definitely* shouldn't get to weasel out," he said. He met his gaze. "We don't need him for this."

"We don't," Orien agreed.

He did it casually and with such speed and skill that Ben didn't realize at first what had happened. Kerill's head thudded onto the floor of the great hall and one of the dinner guests screamed. The three nobles who had been invited by the now-dead host looked at his body and looked away.

The elf was not finished with them, it seemed. He stared at them with a grimly expectant expression.

Slowly, beginning with the three who had supported Kerill, each of the seven heads of household stepped forward to look at the body and turn their hand palm up.

"What does that mean?" Ben muttered to Kule.

"It means they agree that he took what was his due and justice is satisfied," Kule explained. "They agree that he was within his rights."

They might have been reluctant or have hated Orien, but none of them wavered from this. The first of the seven turned to the guards who all waited anxiously.

"Your duties are done," she said. "Guard only your master's property and await the time that an heir is determined." Her tone suggested that she had a hunch of what might happen to Birra. "Let this man and his companions go in peace. They present no danger to the rest of those gathered."

"Thank you," Orien said. He whistled to his soldiers and the group left the room. Ben would have lingered but for the fact that the elf took his arm and pulled him along.

They did not speak until they were out in the darkness and Orien led him to the stables.

"We don't have much time," he said. "You have to go now. Go south of Heffog, sneak past the first town, and take your shelter in the second. The inn barely deserves the name, but it'll do. When we have the information, we'll send for you."

He nodded. "And you?" he asked.

"I don't know," the elf said. "There are many more elven nobles—and some humans—who may face justice in the coming days. I owe it to the people of Heffog to stay through this process. You, though—you're merely a murderer and you need to leave before they find you."

He held his hands out to help him into the saddle.

"You're kidding, right?"

"You know how to ride a horse, surely?"

"Well, yeah, except also *no*."

"Ah." Orien scratched his head. "Well, put your foot here. Just do it. Now, push up and swing your other leg over. One motion. One, two, *three*. There you go."

"Holy shit." He clutched at something to steady himself as the horse pranced nervously. He was much higher up than he had ever imagined being on an animal. "Uh…now what?"

"You'll learn the rest as you go," Orien said simply and smacked the horse's hindquarters with one open palm.

His mount leapt forward. He yelped in alarm and held onto the pommel desperately as the horse cantered into the darkness.

"Now this," Prima said in his head, *"will be hilarious."*

CHAPTER THIRTY

A day and a half later, when the endless parade of medical tests was done and Ben had been fitted for a suit, he sat in a camping chair in a secluded part of Central Park.

On such short notice, Natasha and Mike hadn't arranged a permit for anything in particular, so they had found a small area that wasn't likely to be seen by many passers-by. Much to his surprise, they had asked him to be the minister. Online ordination had been quickly submitted and despite the feeling that this was ridiculous, he had written some comments he could use.

He saw his friend's nod and pushed out of the chair. Mike came to help him to the tiny area they had chosen, now strewn with flower petals. Natasha wore a simple white dress and her hair hadn't been pulled back or dressed up, but she looked radiant. She held a single stem of orchids in one hand.

"Are you sure you can stand?" the man asked him.

"Yep. Not for long, but yep." He planted his feet and smiled at the two of them. "Are you ready?"

"Ready," Mike said with a thumbs-up.

"Ready," Natasha confirmed. She looked like she might explode from happiness.

"Mike and Natasha," Ben said. "For years, the two of you have been a blessing to everyone around you. Every one of our friends turned to you when they had bad luck or loss, and you were always there for them. I think I speak for all of us when I say that I doubted, many times, whether there was anything more to life than disappointment and loneliness, but the example you two set gave me hope."

Mike tilted his head slightly to the side. He knew his friend was surprised. Usually, he wasn't the type to speak about mushy, sentimental things.

But so much had changed recently.

"You may not have known that," he told them, "because I liked to poke fun at you for settling down and being an old married couple. But every time I did that, it was to remind myself that you made it work. I saw you two fight and make up. I saw you disagree and move past it. I saw you hold each other when times were tough. Mike, you were there for Natasha when she lost her job. Natasha, you were there for Mike when his grandfather died, and again when he needed you for everything from eating to deciphering medical statements. The fact that he's standing here now is a testimony to your relationship. Whatever comes your way, I know you'll weather it together."

The couple reached out to clasp each other's hands.

"Do you have your vows?" he asked.

Mike nodded and drew a card from his pocket. "Natasha. Ten years ago, in Introduction to Astronomy, I met the most beautiful woman I had ever seen. It's a good thing I wasn't into Astronomy because you're all I remember from that class. All these years later, every time I look at you, I feel the same way—like I don't know what's down and what's up, and I don't even remember my name."

She laughed and squeezed his hand.

"I promise you," he told her, "that I will be there for you in sickness and in health, for richer and for poorer, in good times and in bad, for the rest of our lives. We've had…uh, well, we've done all that already."

Natasha grinned.

"And I know life will throw other shit at us," he continued. "Wait, am I allowed to swear in these? I guess I'm trying to say I love you and I will always be there for you. We've done it before, and I can think of no one better to share the victories and the good moments with because you make even the worst moments wonderful."

Ben nodded to Natasha.

"Mike." She had memorized her vows and looked into her fiancé's eyes. "I spent a long time trying to think of vows that were better than the traditional ones, and…like you, I kept coming back to them. I swear to love you for better or for worse, in sickness and in health, for richer and for poorer, for the rest of our lives. We are more together than the sum of our parts, and I cannot wait to face both good times and bad with you."

They exchanged rings and murmured the words required after him. Both had tears in their eyes.

"And now," he said, "by the power vested in me by the state of New York and the people at Ministers 'R Us, I pronounce you husband and wife. I'll go sit and you two wait until I'm not looking to make out."

He hobbled to his chair while they laughed. When he stole a glance, they were hugging, her arms gentle around Mike's not completely healed body. They leaned their foreheads together, and he could see their complete comfort in each other's presence.

On the side of the clearing, Nick and DuBois gave him a thumbs-up. They had been drafted as last-minute witnesses and the doctor had offered a reception dinner of popcorn.

Ben's phone buzzed and he pulled it out of his pocket after a few unsuccessful attempts. He smiled when he saw who it was.

How did it go? Eliza had written.

Good. They were basically already married. He looked at his friends. *Now it's merely official. They look so happy.*

I bet you did a great service.

I like to think so. He hesitated. *So, you said you had some news.*

Yeah. I got a job offer to stay here. Good money and way better hours.

That's awesome.

Look, I know this is crazy, but—do you think maybe you'll come back to Colorado?

He tipped his head back to look at the sky. This park was gorgeous, full of greenery and birds chirping, but there was nowhere for him like Colorado—the Rocky Mountains, the Flatirons, the trails and the peaks, the scrub brush, and the sandstone.

I'd like to, he replied cautiously. *But not quite yet. There's more stuff I need to do still. I don't think I'm done with this game yet.* He paused. *Oh, fuck, I need a job. But yeah, I'd like to come back to Colorado. I might even come to Aspen once in a while.*

Well, if you're ever in the area... He could tell she was smiling. *I'll take you out for...not sushi. Not in Aspen. Maybe a steak?*

Actually, I grill a pretty mean steak.

You've got yourself a deal. I'll bring the wine.

He smiled at Natasha and Mike. Grilled steaks. A job. Mountains. For the first time in his life, he wasn't scared of what was coming. He didn't see it as a string of disappointments simply waiting to unfold and was ready for this.

Almost. He was almost ready.